A CHRISTMAS *Renovation*

A Novella

—SMALL TOWN CHRISTMAS—
BOOK 8

❄ ❄ ❄

D. ALLEN

DN Publishing

A Christmas Renovation
Small Town Christmas, Book 8
Copyright © 2023 by D. Allen
Batavia, NY

www.DavidNethBooks.com

ISBN: 978-1-945336-41-6
First Edition

Subscribe to the author's newsletter for updates and exclusive content:
DavidNethBooks.com/Newsletter

Follow the author at:
www.facebook.com/DavidNethBooks

ALSO BY D. ALLEN

MONTANA BEACH
SUMMER STAY

SUMMER JOB

SUMMER NIGHTS

SMALL TOWN CHRISTMAS
A CHRISTMAS REUNION

A CHRISTMAS CHARADE

A CHRISTMAS SPARK

A CHRISTMAS SONG

A CHRISTMAS DEPARTURE

A CHRISTMAS WEDDING

A CHRISTMAS ESCAPE

A CHRISTMAS RENOVATION

STANDALONE
SNOW AFTER CHRISTMAS

November 28th
Cameron

✳ ✳ ✳

"Just about done here, Mrs. Huber." I finish fastening the light fixture back into place. She had three of them to replace, two of which needed to be rewired before I could install them. An easy job that Mr. Huber was perfectly capable of doing himself—as he pointed out several times throughout the day—but Mrs. Huber had insisted that he stay off the ladder.

"You take your time, dear," she tells me from the floor. "I'm impressed that you got it all done by yourself."

I smile politely as I work the screwdriver. If I had a dollar for every time someone made a comment about my capabilities as a contractor because of my gender, I wouldn't need to work in the first place. "Nothing too difficult."

After I had connected the wires, I went down to the basement to turn the breaker back on to double check that everything worked the way it should. Since I wasn't anywhere near the wires when I screwed the fixture back into the ceiling, I didn't bother turning the breaker off again. I probably should have, to be on the safe side, but Mrs. Huber's comments while I worked have been getting to me. Better to get this job done sooner than later.

"Well, we certainly appreciate you coming out," Mrs. Huber says. "Careful coming down the ladder now."

With the light fixture firmly in place, I grab my few tools and descend the ladder. As I near the bottom, I feel Mrs. Huber's hand on my back to steady me. Apparently my anatomy makes me a klutz too.

Gesturing to the light switch, I say, "Give it a shot."

Mr. Huber is quick to come and try it for himself. With the flick of the switch, light illuminates the room.

"Oh, it looks lovely!" Mrs. Huber brings her hands together, just under her chin as she coos.

"Fine work, young lady," Mr. Huber adds.

I offer them both a smile. "Well, let me just clean up my things and I'll be out of your way."

"Your check is in the kitchen," Mrs. Huber says. "Let me go grab it for you."

I kneel down and add my few tools to my toolbox. I have more in the truck, but I like to keep a small box on hand for any projects indoors. Especially in the cold—and wet—Western New York winters.

"Have you been busy with work?" Mr. Huber asks in his wife's absence.

I rock my head back and forth. "Not too bad. This is actually the last job I have lined up until after the holidays."

"At least you'll be able to relax for a while."

Again, I smile. "Yeah." In truth, there will be very little relaxing at all. No work means no money. And as much as it feels good to wrap up one project, what worries me is that I'm still short on the money I need to pay this month's bills *and* be Santa for Angie. I work part-time at a brewery, but those tips are unpredictable. I try not to rely on that money.

"Here you go, dear." Mrs. Huber hands me the check on her return from the kitchen.

"Thank you," I say as we head to the door. "If I don't see you, have a great Christmas."

"You too!" she says.

"Merry Christmas!" Mr. Huber calls. "And enjoy your time off."

I flash him one last smile before exiting the house and hurrying to my truck.

Inside, I turn it on and blast the heat. The radio begins playing Christmas music—"Christmas Time Is Here," from the Charlie Brown's Christmas special—but I turn it down as I study my phone.

There are several texts from my mother. One of them asking what time I'll be done, then another telling me to forget the first text because she remembered the time, then another asking if it would be easier to just have Angie spend the night.

I sigh and type out my reply.

Sorry, just saw this. No, I'll pick up Angie after work tonight. It'll be late, but otherwise I won't get much time with her tomorrow.

My mother's reply is a simple "Ok," to which I reply that I'm on my way to go pick up Angie now. Just after I send the text, though, I get an email from my contractor website about booking my service.

Excitedly, I click the notification and am taken to the automatically-generated email that comes from the submission page.

Name: Lucas Branson

Contact: lukeiamyourfather@gmail.com

Service Needed: General Contracting Work

Date(s) Requested: ASAP

Please give more detail about your project:

Hi, I'm looking to hire a GC for a property I own. It's a family home, but it's in pretty rough shape. Currently a duplex. Looking to make it single-family again. It was built in the early 1900s by my great-grandfather, then was sold out of the family and divided into apartments in the 90s, and I just acquired it last year. I hired a contractor over the summer who did a lot of the demo, but hasn't done much else. The roof and the siding were done in September, but the inside is gutted, other than the apartment upstairs, which I'm currently living in. Hoping to have it livable by Christmas. Let me know if this is something you could work on.

- Luke

It sounds like a doozy, but also one that comes with a higher price point, meaning I could probably charge enough to pay for Angie's Christmas gifts and maybe even a good chunk of next month's bills. Or it would be a steady paycheck if he opted to pay me weekly. Either way, it would bridge the gap between now and the holidays when I will very likely get the calls about plumbing issues.

Glancing up in my rearview mirror, I notice that someone is trying to pull into the Hubers' driveway and I'm in their way. Setting my phone aside, I shift into gear and back out, giving a wave to Nancy Huber as I pass by. We went to school together, albeit she was nearly four years older than me so we didn't cross paths much. Still, we've run into each other several times over the years and we're friendly.

The Hubers live within a three minute drive from

Angie's school, so I decide to head right there. She's somehow made it to fifth grade, meaning that she's at the middle school now. It's hard to believe that my baby girl is already a young lady, but it's true what they say: time waits for no one.

I park on East Avenue, as close as I can to Ross Street, and wait for Angie to come and find me. Each day I pick her up from school to squeeze in extra time with her and each day I'm blown away by how big she's gotten. It seems like it was just yesterday that I found out I was pregnant and went through the messy breakup with her dad, followed by a year of a custody battle, only for him to not follow-through with the promised child support payments. Or the visitations.

I could take him back to court, but what would be the point? He could ask for time with Angie—which he has shown no interest in, ever—and I would get, what? Maybe two hundred dollars from him a month? Not worth it in my book. We've made it by on our own so far. I don't need to bring in anymore stress into our lives, just to make the household checkbook more comfortable.

My phone rings and before I even think about it, I answer it.

"Hello?"

"Hey sweetheart."

My shoulders slump. I thought it might've been a call from a client. Maybe that Lucas Branson guy.

Instead, it's Bryce. My most recent ex.

"Hi." I've learned in the past that it's best to be polite, but curt with him. I've tried rude before, but that just gives him ammunition to talk to me and makes me feel guilty for not hearing him out. If I'm polite, there's no guilt and there's no substance for a conversation either. It's a win-win.

"What are you up to?" he asks.

"Just waiting for Angie."

"For what?"

"To get out of school."

"Oh, is it that time already?"

"Three o'clock," I say. Then, quietly, I add, "Every day."

"Oh. Right. Anyway, I was wondering if you wanted to get dinner tonight. I was thinking we could go out to Stafford to Red Oiser, then maybe on the way back—"

"I have to work tonight."

"Couldn't you just blow it off for tonight?"

"I need the money, Bryce."

He sighs. "I said I'd take care of you. You wouldn't have to work."

I close my eyes and take a deep breath. He has promised that. And truthfully, he is a great guy. Only, he has no interest in kids. Including the one I already have. When we were dating, every time I would talk about Angie or invite him to her school performances or a movie in with the three of us, he would either come up with an excuse not to come or look bored the entire time he was there.

To each their own, so there's no hard feelings with Bryce. But I need to do what's best for me and my daughter because we're a packaged deal. If Bryce doesn't want the whole package then we just wouldn't work out.

"Bryce, we've talked about this," I say.

"I know, I know. I just wanted to leave that little reminder there. But the offer still stands: dinner?"

"I told you, no. I can't."

Another sigh. "Okay. All right, then why don't we make it an early dinner? What time do you have to work? I could drop you off so you don't miss your shift."

"That's sweet," I say, "but I promised Angie we'd watch a Christmas movie together before I have to leave for work." I've been picking up extra shifts at the bar during the week, so I haven't been home. Weeknights have fewer people and fewer tips, but I can't give up my weekends with Angie.

Not to mention, I think my mother would kill me if I had her watch Angie *every* night. She loves her, but every grandma has a limit.

"Tomorrow?"

"I'm working tomorrow night too," I tell him. "Besides, I don't think you and I getting dinner is such a good idea."

"Why not?"

"Because it would blur the lines in our relationship," I tell him. "We ended things in a good way for both of us. Let's not mess that up."

"Well maybe I want to give us another try."

"Then I can bring Angie to dinner?"

"Well…"

"Exactly my point, Bryce. It's fine. I get it. You have the choice to have kids or not. But I don't. I've already made my choice."

There's a pause, then Bryce says, "Okay. I get it. I'll just have dinner for two alone."

I laugh. "At least you have plans."

"Have fun at work. Take care, Cam."

"You too."

By the time I get off the phone, I see the first few kids approach the crosswalk at East and Ross. I watch for a few minutes, keeping my eyes out for my daughter, but don't spot her. Knowing her, she'll be the last one because she stays and chitchats with all of her friends.

Turning back to my phone, I remember that I never replied to that email to Lucas Branson. If I don't reply immediately, there's a chance he'll find another contractor. It's happened before. And by doing business only via email, I often run into people who never reply, so I try not to count my chickens before they hatch.

The price of doing business as a woman.

With an ambiguous name, and the nature of my

industry that calls for me to post my number everywhere, I would *probably* be okay, but I can't take that chance. Something about spreading my contact information out into the world when it's just me and Angie at home doesn't sit right with me. So I only do business via email requests from my website. I'll take a few lost clients if it means keeping our home safe.

Angie spots me down the street and waves goodbye to her friends. She races toward my truck and climbs in. "Hi Mom!"

"Hi honey!" I lean over and give her a hug and a kiss on the top of the head. "How was school?"

"Good! Are we going back to watch the movie?"

"You bet. I don't have to work until eight and then Grandma will be over to hang out with you before bed."

She nods, but is quiet as I pull away from the curb.

"What's the matter?" I ask.

"I wish you didn't have to work two jobs."

As I fight back the emotion that threatens to overtake me, I simply say, "I do too, sweetheart."

November 29th
Luke

❄ ❄ ❄

"Are you sure you can't squeeze this project in?" I hold my phone to my ear as I pace around the remnants of the stately living room in my family's home. I just reacquired it at an auction back in the spring and have spent most of the year trying to work with a lousy contractor. He was always looking for shortcuts or had excuses not to do something, and he was never able to keep to his promised deadlines. But he never had trouble spending my money. I had no choice but to let him go last month.

Adam, on the other end of the phone, laughs. "This isn't a project that just gets squeezed in, Luke. Nor would you want me to if I could. What you're looking for is a *restoration*, not your typical *renovation*."

I groan. "I know. But since I fired my contractor I'm sitting on an empty house that isn't progressing anywhere."

"But it's where you live."

"I have to, in order to be able to afford the back taxes," I say. "*And* save up for the costs to fix this place. Not to mention maintaining all of my other properties." I lean against the oak pillar separating the living room from the dining room. It had been a battle to get the former contractor to keep it. "I'm out of my wheelhouse with this one. I'm used to paying people to do simple flips, squeeze in as many apartments as possible, and either rent them out or sell the whole building."

"And now you need to slow down and take your time," Adam tells me. "I'm just not the guy who can help you. Fortunately, I'm booked for the winter."

I'm glad to hear that. My friend deserves to have a steady income stream, but it still doesn't help me any.

"Have you tried calling around to other contractors?" Adam suggests.

"I've been contacting people like crazy! Either everyone's booked or they need a few weeks before they can start. I promised my parents that I could host Christmas here!"

"That's probably not going to happen."

"Don't remind me. Honestly, I think they'll be okay if just the living room is done, so we can put up the tree and have that nostalgic feeling and all, but at this point I'm thinking they'd be better off if they just stayed in Florida and didn't see this place in the state that it's in."

"They'll get over it and so will you," Adam says. "Don't stress too much about it. You've put out feelers, now see if any of them take you up on the job. If not, it's not like the house is going anywhere. You can tackle it after the holidays."

Again, I groan. "That's not the way it was supposed to go."

"Sometimes life doesn't go according to plan." He chuckles, then adds, "Actually, *mostly* life doesn't go according to plan. Good luck."

"I'll talk to you later."

After hanging up, I check my messages. Nothing. No voicemails. No texts. No emails.

"Ugh, I wish *somebody* would get back to me," I murmur.

Not being able to take the stillness in the house, I lock up and head out to my car to check on some of my other properties in the area.

Every week I make my rounds to all of my properties. I own two outside of town. One is a farmstead, where I double-dip by renting out the large house to two different families, while also collecting an income from boarding horses and running a small horse-riding camp in the summer. One of the renters in the main house loves horses, so takes that up as her job in the summer when she's not teaching. It's a win-win.

"Hi Marcy! I'm just checking in," I say when she answers the door.

She steps aside and says, "Come in."

I follow her in, but linger on the small shoe mat by the door. My shoes are covered in mud and snow — I'll have to wipe them clean in the car. "How's everything going? Need anything?"

"I have to order more food for the horses. Did you want me to have the company charge it to the card on file? I don't know if their prices have increased, but I could ask for an invoice if you want."

"If you could, that would be great. Depending on how much it goes up, I may have you shop around a bit for other providers."

Marcy leans back against the kitchen counter. The room is small, and doubles as both a place where her family prepares food, as well as a hallway between the living room and the dining room. The original house was huge when I bought it, so the square footage allowed me to slice it up into two apartments.

"Oh. Okay."

"Is there something wrong?" I ask.

She shakes her head. "No. Not really. It's just that, the horses are used to that type of food and I'd rather not change their diet when they're already not getting out and riding as much in the colder months.

Besides, right now we order from a local farmer. If he's raising his rates, it's only because the cost of doing business is going up for him too."

I nod. "I understand that, but I'm running a business as well. I need to watch out for my costs too. That means making sure I'm always getting the best price."

Marcy still doesn't seem convinced. "It's just that, over the years, he's become a good friend. And if I tell him that we're no longer ordering from him, then…" She trails off, but the end of her sentence is clear enough.

"He should be mature enough to separate business and personal connections," I say. "I'm sure your friendship will survive." I turn toward the door. "Well, if there's anything you need, give me a call. Merry Christmas."

She offers a polite smile and follows me to the door. "Yes, thank you. Merry Christmas to you too."

Out in the car, I grab a rag from the trunk and wipe off the mud and dirt from the bottoms of my shoes. This is always my least-favorite stop for this reason.

I've considered selling them place several times, but whenever I bring it up to Marcy, she convinces me not to. If I sold it and the new owners didn't want to keep the horses, then they would have to be sold as well. So far Marcy has persuaded me to keep it, but if costs keep going up, then I'll have no choice but to let it go. It's a shame, but I could get a two-unit house in town that pays the same amount of rent for significantly less work.

The other property out of town is another summer property on Horseshoe Lake. It's a little cottage just across the street from the water, which brings the value down a little, but with housing rentals being on the rise, it actually makes a decent profit. And it was another property bought at auction, meaning that the only thing I owe on it are the property taxes and insurance, both of which are made up from weekly rentals from out-of-towners.

After checking on both of those properties and checking in with the tenants at the farmstead, I head back into town to survey the progress going on at the two other flips I have going on.

The first one is on Montclair Avenue. It's a more transitional part of town, where depending on the end of the street the property is depends on whether it's a good neighborhood or a bad one. Luckily, that's changing, meaning that my flip of a duplex closer to La Cross Avenue is projected to turn a profit once it's finished. Assuming that it will be completed on time.

"How's everything going?" I ask when I walk in the front door of the lower unit.

The contractor greets me with a handshake, then indicates the paper on the floor so we're mindful of our messy feet on the new flooring. Simple and cheap EVP that looks like hardwood but is more durable for the tenants coming and going. Even though my leases always state that the tenant should maintain the home as best as possible, they rarely do.

"Not bad. We're just finishing up a few punch-list things," Collin tells me. "Hey, I wanted to show you something while you're here." He leads me through the tight apartment and back to one of the bedrooms that was created from what was once the formal dining room in the original layout of the house. "We've got this staircase here that we don't need anymore. Taking it out is going to push back the schedule and take more labor, but it'd free up some space in this room. What do you think?"

I look around the room. "It's already plenty big enough."

"Yeah, but it doesn't have a closet. Taking out the stairs would give us the space to create a closet."

Again, I survey the space. Briefly, my thoughts drift to my own house. If the contractor who had converted it to a duplex in the 90s had taken out key features, the opportunity to restore it would be slimmer, if not impossible. Better to have to remove walls to expose the original layout than to have to recreate special features completely.

I shake my head. "Just leave the stairs. Frame it in and add a bar. There. You have a closet with built-in shelving."

Collin raises his eyebrows. "You sure you want to do that? It's pretty shoddy work."

I wave it off. "If someone complains, then they don't need to rent from me. Just go ahead and do it."

"If you say so, boss."

I start to head out of the room, then stop and turn back to him. "Hey, give me a call with an update by the end of the week. Hopefully we can have this place wrapped up before Christmas and rented out by the first of the year."

Collin gives one quick nod. "Will do."

"Thanks."

I step back out into the cold and head to the car for the next property, which is in more or less the same shape. Almost complete, should be rented by the first of the year. After I check on that one, I'll run and grab coffee, then check the auction page and the MLS to scout out my next investment. My ads for the rentals in the city are already running, so I'll have to check my email for inquiries about those as well.

Before I drive off to the final property, I hear my phone ding with a message.

Perfect, I think to myself. *These houses will be rented in no time.*

But it isn't from a potential renter. It's from someone named Cameron Kutcher. The name doesn't ring a bell, but based on the subject line he's obviously replying to an email I sent. Probably the inquiry about working on my family's home.

Re: General Contracting Work

Hi Luke,

Your project sounds like a challenge, but also sounds fun. I would love to check it out. I just finished up a job, so I could come as early as today (11/29) or tomorrow (11/30) if you want. I'll take a look, see if it's something I could handle in your timeframe, and then let you know a potential cost—although I can be flexible with that to help fit your budget.

Let me know what time works for you and the address, and I'll see you there. Thanks!

- Cameron Kutcher

A properly-spelled email from a contractor? I'm already impressed. But, honestly, even if the email was riddled with typos and misspellings, the fact that I got a reply from someone at all—especially one who is able to start immediately—takes the choice right out of my hands.

Re: Re: General Contracting Work

Great! If you could stop out today (11/29) around 1:00, that'd be great. I'm ready to get started on this!

- Luke

In the post-script, I include the address and my phone number, in case he has trouble finding it. From the outside, the house looks like it fits right in with the neighboring houses, but inside is a whole different story. Sometimes it's hard to find.

With an extra pep in my step, I start the car, shift into gear, and head off to my next property.

The day is off to a great start.

November 29th
Cameron

❄ ❄ ❄

When I had written in the email that I was free as early as today, I had really been hoping that Luke Branson would choose tomorrow. In fact, it wasn't until after I had sent that email that the reminder on my phone pinged about Angie's parent-teacher conference.

It was supposed to be the week of Thanksgiving but I had to cancel it at the last minute because I got called in for an emergency plumbing issue. The rescheduled visit had completely slipped my mind. Luckily, her teacher is able to squeeze me in during her lunch break today, but with meeting Luke Branson at 1:00, that doesn't leave me a lot of time. Hopefully I won't have to rush through it.

"Mrs. Simpson?" I ask as I step into the classroom. "I'm sorry I'm a little early. Is this okay?"

She wipes away crumbs from her desk and nods as she gets up. She takes an extra second to finish chewing, then extends her hand out to me.

"Sorry. This is actually perfect timing. I just took the kids down to lunch. I thought I could squeeze in mine before you came."

I cringe. "I'm sorry. Feel free to eat while we talk." I glance at my watch. "I've actually got another meeting at 1:00 today that's come up last minute."

Mrs. Simpson motions to a table at the back of the classroom. "Have a seat. I'll grab Angie's folder." She returns to her desk momentarily and comes back with a manilla folder.

"I just want to say that Angie loves school this year," I tell her as she takes the seat beside me. "She's never been happier. And she seems to be learning a lot."

She smiles. "I'm glad to hear that. She's doing spectacularly. All of her grades are excellent. She has a good group of friends—although they tend to get out of hand from time to time. But they're ten, and they're still kids. That's bound to happen."

I try to tone down my excitement, but I'm beaming with pride in my daughter.

"My only concern is her penmanship," Mrs. Simpson goes on. "We've done so much with computers that a lot of students struggle with this, but it's important that she strengthen these skills as well. We're working on having her slow down while she's writing and try to build up those muscles in her hand to keep her writing longer and neater." She passes me an example of Angie's handwriting, which I already know looks like chicken scratch. As a matter of fact, so does mine. But I can clean it up when I need to.

I nod. "Okay. Is there anything I can do at home to help with this?"

"Well, after Christmas break, I'm going to be assigning more handwritten homework, just so the kids can practice their writing. I'd encourage you to keep an eye on her when she's completing the work and remind her to slow down and write as neatly as she can. Over time it will become more natural to her."

"That sounds reasonable."

Mrs. Simpson smiles. "Trust me, this isn't a major concern, but an area that she can work on. Angie is a wonderful girl and I love having her in class."

I smile again, still bursting with pride. "I'm glad to hear that."

After the meeting, I hurry out of the school and down the front steps, careful not to slip on any unsuspecting ice that has accumulated.

As I rush to my car, I kick myself for trying to look nice for the parent-teacher conference. If it wasn't for these heeled boots, I'd be moving a lot faster. For half a second, I consider changing my footwear in the truck, but decide against it. I don't have the time and I would look absolutely ridiculous in work boots and nice black slacks. Not that the guy hiring me would probably care, but still. First impressions and all.

I race down Washington Avenue, grateful that the school and the house I'm looking for are simply at opposite ends of a long street.

When I finally turn onto Ellicott Avenue, I slow and turn the radio down so I can see the house numbers better. As I crawl down the street in my truck, my eyes flash between the email from Luke Branson on my phone and the houses I slowly pass by.

As soon as I spot it, I jerk the truck to the side of the street and park it, turn the keys, and slip out of the truck with my trusty notepad and pen in hand.

From the outside, the house doesn't look too bad. It makes me wonder what kind of structural horrors there are on the inside.

I knock on the front door and wait in the chilly winter breeze until the large oak entrance finally swings open.

"Hello?" The man who answers is cute, albeit a little stuffy. He's wearing khakis and a powder blue button-down shirt with a crimson tie.

"Hi, I'm here for a meeting with Lucas Branson," I say. "Are you him?"

His eyes narrow. "Ye-Yes — I'm sorry, but this isn't the house I'm trying to rent. I have one I can show you around the corner on Montclair."

I pull out my phone and check the address, then glance at the house number above the door. "No, this is definitely the right place."

He shakes his head and starts to retreat into the house, grabbing at the door behind him. "You must be mistaken. This property is nowhere near ready to rent."

I press my hand against the door to keep it open. "I'm not looking to rent. *You* reached out to me."

That boggles his mind even further. "I don't solicit tenants via email."

I bite my bottom lip in an effort to keep in any snark. "I'm not looking to *rent*. I'm looking to renovate." I glance inside as best I can. "Or rather, restore."

"Oh. I didn't…" He trails off as he pulls out his phone to check his notes.

"My name's Cameron Kutcher." I extend my hand toward him.

Slowly, he reaches out and takes it. "Oh. Oh! I'm sorry. I wasn't — I didn't — I'm sorry."

I smile. He had no idea I'd be a woman. That happens more often than it should, but construction is a man's business typically. "Do you mind if I come in out of the cold?"

"Oh, sure. Yes!" He steps aside and allows me to

enter. "Can't say it's much warmer in here, though. I try not to waste money on heating when there's nobody down here."

"Be careful not to keep it too cold," I say as I look around. The house has seen better days. Plaster is cracking. Wallpaper's peeling. Floorboards are buckling. But it has charm. And elegance, under all the dirt and dust. "Especially if there's nobody down here very often. If the pipes freeze and break, you'll have a hell of a mess to clean up."

He nods. "Trust me, I know. I've been in real estate long enough to know those kinds of basics." He points to the tall ceilings, which reverberate our voices back to us in this empty cavern. "I live upstairs. There's a small apartment that uses some of the same systems as the ones for down here and I check on this unit frequently."

"You said in your email that you want to make it single-family again?" I raise my notepad to jot down his plans.

He nods. "Yeah. Eventually. If it makes more sense, I can move out and we can tear up that apartment upstairs if you'd rather do it all at once."

I rock my head back and forth. "Depends on how they've chopped it up. Some people have been ruthless, especially with these large old houses. They just cut and chop whatever they want to squeeze in another unit or an extra bedroom to charge more in rent."

Luke's quiet at first, then says, "My intent is to live here when it's all done. It's a family home that I've recently reacquired."

"You said you want to get some of it done before Christmas?"

He nods. "Yeah. As much as possible. I promised my folks I'd have it ready to spend the holiday here as a family."

I slowly make my way around the large living room. Surprisingly, there's a lot of the original woodwork is still intact. "What work has been done so far?"

"I hired someone this past summer to work on some stuff outside," he explains. "Repainting, insulating for the winter, that kind of stuff. It cost way too much and took way too long that I had to let him go. I had every intent to let him do the whole house, but after taking two months to paint and replace the roof, and then it costing me double what he quoted?" He shakes his head. "I could tell I was getting ripped off."

"Well, if you hire me, I'll try to get you a fair price, but it needs to be worthwhile for me as well. Plus, this house needs some money invested in it to bring it back to its full potential." I wave my pen at the ceiling. "All that plaster work is going to take time and money."

"Just drywall over it."

I shake my head. "Are we going for cheap or authentic here?"

Luke seems to be taken aback. "Uh…authentic, I guess."

"Then we need to stay as true to the house's original structure as possible. We can do drywall on the ceilings because it'll be hard to tell from down here since they're so tall, but all along the border and the walls and everything—those will need to be plastered. And if you're thinking about taking down all the plaster to drywall, then we're talking hours and hours of labor, not to mention the dust, which could result in you losing some of these things you want to keep." I step over and pat the wooden window casing. All of them seem to be in perfect condition. "Please tell me you're keeping these."

"As much as I can. I was thinking about painting them white to brighten up the place, but I don't know."

I'm shaking my head before he finishes. "If you paint these beautiful oak pieces, you'd be spitting in the faces of the carpenters who slaved away at these and all the generations of people who enjoyed them. If you want to brighten up the place, get some extra lamps."

"And pay the extra in the utility bill?"

"Another lamp is going to cost you pennies per month to run," I counter. "Painting the wood is irreversible. But hey, if you're looking for a quick, cheap fix, then that's fine. I'm just not the girl for you or this project then. I'll walk right out that door right now."

Luke stares at me, surprised. Then a smile spreads across his face. "You're passionate about this stuff, aren't you?"

"It's my life's work. Literally."

We both laugh.

"Seriously," I go on, "I would love to be in a position to buy up old houses like this, do a full restoration to bring each house back to what it was meant to look like, and then sell it to a homeowner who is going to appreciate it and love it and take care of it for years to come."

"So why don't you?"

I shrug. "Honestly? Money. I never have enough cash flow to buy the house, and hire a team of people to help me work on it. And managing all of that on my own while my income is frozen? That'd be a nightmare. Besides, I don't know anything about selling houses. Just fixing them."

"Well, you've certainly impressed me, that's for sure."

I smile, then look around the room again. "You want to get as much of this done before Christmas?"

He nods. "That's the plan."

I shake my head. "That's not going to happen. At least, not *well*. I can promise to have the living room done in time, although doing each room at a time will be a bit of a pain. These floorboards should be a simple fix and if the place is insulated, then half of that work is done for you. Plus your utilities all work just fine if you have that apartment upstairs. If we need to update them, we can do that after the holidays. We'll just have to be careful with this room after the first of the year when we're working on the other parts of the house."

"Sounds like you won't have too hard a time managing a team."

"I know what needs to be done and the order to do it in."

He leads me to the door. "I like that confidence."

"Let me go home and figure out a quote for you. I can send you an email in a couple hours and we can go from there."

Luke shakes his head. "No need. As long as your quote isn't outrageous, I'd love to hire you for this project. I can get the paperwork drawn up by the end of the day and have it emailed to you."

I can't help but smile. "Thank you! I'm looking forward to working on this one! It's a beautiful house and it sounds like you have a deep connection to it."

"I do. How soon can you start? Tomorrow?"

My eyebrows raise in surprise, but I also feel relief. "Absolutely!"

November 30th
Luke

❄ ❄ ❄

Early the next morning, I'm down in the main part of the house standing on a ladder and pinning tarps over the doorways to keep any dust and debris out of the rest of the house.

My next stop is to pick up coffee for Cameron and whoever she brings with her to help work.

That's the extent of my construction skills. Assisting. I used to feel ashamed about it, but at the end of the day, as the landlord and owner of each property, the checks continue to come to me even after the construction crews have moved out, so it's helped me get over my own ego.

The knock at the door pulls me out of my head. As I descend the ladder, I call out, "It's open!"

Cameron walks in—alone—with her toolbox in one

hand and a cup of coffee in the other. She wears a tattered green hoodie that's covered in paint stains and her jeans have holes in the knees, like they've been worn naturally and not like she bought them like that. Certainly a different look from yesterday.

She smiles at me. "Good morning! I'm ready to get started."

"Morning," I reply. "I was hoping you and I could really quickly run through what the final plan is before you get started."

"The final plan? I suppose I could draw up blueprints, but we're not moving walls or doors or windows or anything. I didn't think blueprints were necessary. And that would delay everything…"

I shake my head. "No, I know that. I wasn't expecting blueprints. Just a final scope of work. Not that I come in one day and am surprised that you moved something or painted over something I wanted to keep."

That's happened in the past. If you don't stay on top of contractors, they tend to go hog-wild.

"Sure, we can walk through it. But I promise you, I wouldn't make any changes without checking with you first."

"I appreciate that, but I've been told that in the past," I respond. "To be honest, I'm a little gun-shy when it comes to you people."

She raises her eyebrows. "You people?"

"Contractors."

"Ah." She nods. "I suppose that's better than other stereotypes I've been grouped with." With her drink, she motions to the fireplace that centers the room. "You want to start here? What are your thoughts on the fireplace?"

"I want to keep it."

"Well, obviously, but do you want it to be functional?" She sets her drink on the mantle and crouches down to peer into the flue. Without any gloves, she reaches up into it and pulls out a wad of insulation, that brings down dust, leaves, and other debris with it.

Good thing I hung up the sheets.

"Do you think it's functional?" I ask.

"Definitely not right now." She pulls a small flashlight from her back pocket and peers deep inside the fireplace. "I can't really see much. I'll have to wait until the dust settles. And even then, we'd probably have to hire a fireplace expert to check it out. But I'm willing to bet that you don't have a cap on the chimney up on the roof. Didn't you say they replaced the roof this summer?"

When she pulls away from the fireplace, there's dust and soot on her face. She wipes it away with the sleeve of her hoodie and doesn't seem to mind that it's only smeared.

"I did," I say as I let out a breath. "But is all that necessary? Wouldn't it be easier to just close it off?"

"Well, the cap on the roof is absolutely

necessary—assuming you don't have one. I could see if I have a ladder tall enough and go up and check on that later. The cap is going to keep water and leaves and even birds out of your chimney—as best as it can while still allowing smoke out."

"And if I close it up?"

"Then you won't need to let smoke out. But you'd lose the ambiance of the fireplace." She shrugs. "It's up to you. There are ways you can dress up the fireplace if it's closed up, so you don't lose that ambiance. If you really wanted, we could try to install a gas or electric insert, but sometimes those don't look quite right and we'd have to drill a hole through the bricks to run the line, which would mean taking off the plaster from above the mantle. That'll create more mess and take more time. Besides, if it's nostalgia you're going for, you might want to invest in a proper update to the whole system so you can have a traditional wood-burning fire. Of course, that will also have maintenance costs every year."

"How much is all of this going to cost right now?"

"Depends on what the fireplace expert says and what kind of fireplace you want in the end."

I rub my forehead. "And all of this is on top of the quote we discussed?"

She makes a face. "Unfortunately."

"And you waited until now to ask me about this? You couldn't have brought it up yesterday when you saw the house?" The tone of my voice is accusatory, but it's only because I see dollar bills flying out of my wallet with each passing moment. And she's only been here ten minutes.

"You asked me to do a restoration," she says. "My hope is to maintain the integrity of the house without cutting corners. In order to do that I need to make sure everything is up to code as well, while also making it look timeless and like it was never in disrepair in the first place. Not to mention the fact that I want to make sure that *you're* happy with it as well. That's all going to take time and money."

"You agreed you'd have it done by Christmas."

"The living room, not any other part of the house. That'll take longer, but we can discuss that later."

"You don't think there's any chance of you getting to the kitchen—or even a bathroom—before Christmas too?"

She barks out a laugh, then covers her mouth. "Sorry. But that's just not going to happen."

I huff out a sigh and cross my arms. "So what *are* you going to get done?"

"The living room. Like I promised you yesterday."

That answer doesn't sit well with me. I can just picture Mom making a comment about how it's "almost" like when she was younger. And "too bad" we couldn't get rid of the tarps. Or Dad complaining about the state of the yard or the dust creeping in from behind the tarps.

Still, Cameron had said from the beginning that she was only going to get to the living room, so I don't really have an argument. But I still don't like it.

"Look," she says after a second, "I'm not going to lie to you about the timeline. I'm also not going to take advantage of you. I get it that you're nervous about contractors, but I think it's because in the past you've had people over-promise and under-deliver. If anyone tells you they can get this whole house done in a matter of weeks, then they're either lying through their teeth or they're cutting so many corners that this house won't meet code."

I stare at the floor, not liking what I'm hearing but having no rebuttal. She's spot on. I've hired terrible contractors in the past because they were cheap. And those bad decisions have put me in a not-so-great place currently. If I'm going to get this house back to the way it was, I'm going to need Cameron's help. She seems to know what she's doing. Now I just need to trust her.

"Okay," I say. "You're right. I get it. But help me out here. Keep me in the loop when it comes to any extra expenses. Don't take me for a ride. If I don't need something, I don't want it."

"Of course. I wouldn't take advantage of you like that. I have a reputation to keep as a contractor in town. Besides, Batavia is where I live. I want to see every house looking its best. I'm not going to skimp on any of my projects."

"I appreciate that—and I believe you have good intentions. But it's still hard for me to give up control on a project that's so meaningful to me. Especially when you're talking about things that I don't understand."

She nods. "I get it. This is your baby. It's where your family grew up. I'll try to walk you through everything that needs to be done. And listen, today I'm going to go around and make a list of everything I need from the hardware store. I was planning on going out tomorrow to get a lot of the materials and order anything I can't get immediately. You're more than welcome to tag along."

"Yes. Of course. I'll be there."

Cameron grins. "Good."

DECEMBER 1ST
Cameron

❄ ❄ ❄

When I pull up to the house, Luke is already waiting out front. I roll down the window with the window crank and lean my head out.

"Get in, loser! We're going shopping." I flash him a smile so he knows I'm joking. As he comes around to get in the passenger side, I use my sleeve to clear off the snow that's fallen all over the inside door of the truck.

"That was the dumbest line I've ever heard," he says when he gets in.

"Admit it, you laughed." I shift into gear and back down the driveway and onto the street.

"Are you sure this truck is safe? Looks like it's about thirty years old."

"Maybe technically, but I swear I've replaced every

part on this thing at least three times in the ten years that I've had it." I pat the dash. "This is my first."

He raises his eyebrows.

"My first car." The truck shakes as we make our way over the bumps in the road on Mix Place as we head toward Oak Street. "Geez, get your mind out of the gutter. Anyway, how are we paying for everything today?"

"What do you mean?"

"The store is going to expect currency in exchange for goods." I'm in a good mood today. Despite our tiff yesterday morning, the day had gone pretty well. And the fact that I have a job until at least Christmas, possibly longer, means that I no longer have to worry about where my next paycheck is coming from. And Luke is easy to talk to. "Am I putting everything on the company card and billing you through an invoice or did you want to pay for it all yourself and only pay me for my services?"

"Which would be easier?"

I shrug. "Doesn't matter." We get to the light at Oak and Park and I turn onto Park toward the big box stores on the edge of town.

"Let's see how much the bill comes to."

A few minutes later, I'm pulling the truck into a parking spot near the contractor's entrance of Home Depot. Stretching around, I grab my clipboard with my notes from yesterday from the backseat.

"Ready?" I ask.

Luke gets out of the truck and we walk quickly through the chilly air and into the store. It doesn't take long to see that Luke is in a whole different world from what he's used to. His neck cranes as he looks around at the many signs all around.

"This way." I lead him down toward the plaster materials and begin looking around for what I need.

Luke, meanwhile, studies the labels of different products and then sets each down carefully, as if afraid that he might break something.

"Hmm," I murmur. "I think I'm going to need a cart for everything we need. Do you mind going to grab one? They should be up near the registers."

"Sure thing." He walks to the end of the aisle and then looks both ways, as if he's lost. Finally, his eyes lock on the registers and he walks away in that direction.

I can't help but smile and roll my eyes. Somehow, his ignorance to all things construction makes him that more adorable.

In his absence, I actually get more done. I'm able to grab whatever items I need without the worry of having to justify its cost to Luke. But after nearly ten minutes without Luke returning, I grow a little worried and head out in search of him.

He's standing among the Christmas trees, right near the main entrance. His eyes seem lost in the twinkling light and grandeur of the tall, artificial, evergreens.

"This wasn't on my list, but I'll gladly haul it back to the house for you in my truck." I set my items in the cart, grateful to be relieved of the weight.

He's startled by my presence and seems flustered as he maneuvers the cart back toward the main aisle. "I was…I was just looking. Yeah."

"It's okay. These trees are beautiful. Are you an artificial guy or a real guy?"

Luke's eyebrows scrunch together in confusion. "Huh?"

I point. "The Christmas tree. Real or fake?"

"Oh! Uh, fake I guess. The only time I ever had a real one, my dad didn't tighten the screw tight enough at the bottom and it was leaning for weeks. Then, right before my family arrived on Christmas Eve, the whole thing fell over." He chuckles and shakes his head. "There was a mess. Water spilled everywhere, pine needles all over the floor. My mother wasn't happy that several of the ornaments shattered. But she tells that same story every year."

"That's a nice memory."

"What about you? Real or fake?"

I shrug. "Fake. Buying a new tree every year was not in our budget, so a fake one as a one-time purchase was ideal. But I always thought it would be nice to go out and get a real tree. Make a day out of it. Smell the pine scent all season long." I reach for the pine scents from the shelf and pass them to Luke. "But that's what these are for."

He laughs. "These pale in comparison to the real thing."

"Meh, they've sufficed my whole life." I nudge him out of the way and direct the cart back toward the main part of the store. "Okay. Let's get back to the real reason we're here."

The rest of the shopping trip goes surprisingly smoothly. Luke doesn't question any of my other purchases. He balks at the price of each, but quickly admits that it's the cost of construction. One that has been rising significantly in recent years. At the register, he doesn't hesitate at all to pull out his wallet and swipe his credit card through.

"You sure you don't want me to run it through the business?" I ask just before he finishes the purchase.

"Nah. I'll pay for it anyway. Might as well get the points for it. Besides, it'll save you the hassle of having to itemize all of that."

Construction materials might be outside of his realm of knowledge, but budgets and accounting were certainly not. Which was good, because that's where my skills lacked. Thank God for my mother for keeping track of the books for the business.

Out in the parking lot, the snow is coming down in heavy, wet flakes. The kind that melt as soon as they touch you and cause you to be chillier from the dampness.

We load up the back of the truck. Luke helps me load up the lumber and other large items. We both pile in the cab of the truck and brush the snow off of us.

"Woo!" Luke cries out. "It's chilly."

"It's damp," I counter. "But yes, chilly." I fire up the truck and head back out toward the city.

We're quiet as I drive. Both of us seem captivated by the falling snow and the changing landscape around us as everything is blanketed in white.

As we approach the intersection with Richmond Avenue, I turn on my signal to turn left and start to veer into the turning lane, but Luke speaks up.

"No, go straight."

"Why?" I turn off my signal and pass through the light. If I wanted, I could take Mix Place up ahead to Ellicott Avenue and be at the house in the same amount of time, so the detour doesn't really matter.

"I want to buy you a coffee," he says. "I tried yesterday but you already had your own."

"It's my morning ritual," I say. "And I know what you're going to say about that, so don't even."

"What am I supposedly going to say?"

"If I bought myself a cup of coffee every morning, it adds up to be thousands of dollars a year, which I could be putting toward more useful things."

He waves it off. "Do what makes you happy. If coffee in the morning helps you get through the day, then by all means drink coffee. There are other ways to save money too."

My eyes widen in surprise. "Wow. I didn't think

you'd say that." We turn onto Main Street and pass by a Dunkin' on the other side of the median. "Should I turn around? Or did you want to go to Tim Horton's up here?"

Luke points and says, "There's a local place on Harvester. We should go there."

"You venture all the way down to Harvester for coffee?"

He shrugs. "Sometimes."

Surprise after surprise after surprise.

Still, I take us down to Harvester Avenue and park on the street in front of the massive building. It used to be a huge industrial plant a long time ago. Now, it houses small businesses and other start-ups.

We get out and walk along the sidewalk against the building, both of us burying our hands in our pockets and shrugging our shoulders up against the wind. With the large building, it creates a sort of wind tunnel that seems to whip right through all of my layers.

Inside, we order our drinks and then Luke takes a seat in one of the lounge chairs in the corner. I stand nearby, but he motions to the chair.

"Have a seat."

"Shouldn't we get back to the house so I can get to work?"

"Take a moment to relax," he says. "I thought we could talk."

Confused, I take a seat and wait for him to initiate

the conversation. I don't mind talking to him, but I'm not sure what exactly he's getting at right now.

"How are you?" he asks.

"I'm okay. Do you do this with all of your contractors?"

"No, you're the first."

I sit up, suddenly flushed with anger. "Is it because I'm a woman?"

"Order up!" the barista calls from the counter.

Luke rushes up to grab our cups and then returns with them. I take a careful sip and savor the rich flavor and warmth radiating through my body.

I'm quiet, waiting for his answer.

He seems to relish in the silence.

"I'm waiting," I tell him.

"No, it's not because you're a woman," he says. "It's because I've had bad luck with contractors in the past and I thought having a more personal connection would mean that they'd be less likely to screw me over. I've been listening to this podcast about how you can only control your actions, so I thought—"

"You could schmooze me by wining and dining me so I don't steal your wallet and ride off into the sunset?"

He grins. "Something like that."

"What else is this podcast teaching you?"

He bristles. "I don't know if it's *teaching* me anything, so much as reminding me of stuff I already know. The whole gist of the podcast is to be nice to people and you'll get nice things in return. Most of the time. So I just wanted to reach out to you and extend an olive branch, of sorts."

"Isn't an olive branch for when you've wronged someone and you're trying to make amends?"

"Why are you trying to make this so difficult?" he asks with a chuckle. "I thought I'd do something nice and get you a coffee to show my appreciation for you and how quickly you've been able to take on this project. Can't that coffee come with a little conversation as well?"

I lean back in my seat with my cup in my hands. "Well, even though I haven't really done anything on your house yet other than spend your money, consider me appreciated."

Luke cocks his head to the side. "Oh. Good point. I didn't think about how you haven't done anything yet. Maybe I should take that drink back." He starts to reach for it, but I pull away.

"No!"

"Then maybe you should pay your way."

I take a sip and look at him over the rim. "I'm too busy feeling appreciated."

"So it's working then?"

I reach for his hand to make sure I have his attention. "I promise, I will not screw you over like the other contractors."

"Good."

DECEMBER 15TH
Luke

* * *

When I step into the house, Cameron turns off the belt sander for the floors and then pulls down her mask. "Careful. It's dusty. This is usually a summertime project, but I assumed you'd probably kill me if I decided to open a window. I blocked off the air ducts as much as possible, though." She motions to the vents under the windows.

"You are right in that assumption." The smell of sawdust fills the air, but it doesn't bother me too much. I hand her a cup of coffee. "This is for you. Sorry it's late."

She pulls off her gloves and takes the cup from me. "Thanks."

Ever since I made a big stink about getting her coffee last week, she hasn't been coming to the job site with one of her own. At least, not that I've seen anyway. It's been a way for me to show her my appreciation for everything she's doing, besides the paycheck I'm giving her.

"This place has come a long way," I say as I look around.

She puts her hands on her hips and takes it in herself. "It's getting there."

"How's everything coming?"

She takes in a deep breath. "It's a bit of a disaster, isn't it? I was hoping I could get the floors sanded today so I can stain by the end of the day so they can set overnight, but some of these water stains are deeper than I thought and it's going to take a little more work. I think I'm going to be here late today."

"Don't kill yourself over this."

Cameron pulls out her phone from the front of her jeans. "Thanks for the sentiment, but if we don't stay on schedule, there's no way you'll be in here by Christmas. And I intend to keep my promise to have this place ready by the holidays."

"Do you need more manpower?"

She shakes her head as she taps away on her phone. "More people won't help. I need the space cleared so I can do the floors. What I need is more time."

"Can't help you there."

"Hence my dilemma." She points up at the ceiling at the chandelier with the crumbling decorative plaster around it. "The light fixture is fixed. I have a guy coming in a couple days to work on that medallion and to touch up a couple things."

"You can't do it yourself?"

"Plaster is an art form. And I want this place in tip-top shape. Don't worry. It's all within budget."

"That's what I like to hear."

"The fireplace guy was out here on Monday," she goes on. "He says it's fully-functional and he took care of everything that it needed up on the roof. I could bore you with the technical details, but—"

"But I'd rather just know if I can use it or not. And the bill. How much did that set me back?"

"Cheaper than we both thought. With the contingency you factored in, I think we can stay in budget."

"That's good." I feel a weight lift from my shoulders. "What's the status on the tiles by the hearth?"

She walks over and kneels beside them. "They look to be in pretty good shape to me. There are a few cracks, but nothing appears to be loose. I suppose I could replace them if you wanted to update them, but—"

"But I'd rather not spend the money and you'd rather keep the integrity of the house."

She smiles and looks down at the half-sanded floor. "Exactly."

We're finishing each other's sentences now. How

easily the two of us have clicked in the short time she's been working for me.

Cameron's phone dings. She pulls it out and reads it. "Shoot."

"What's the matter?"

She sighs heavily and stares at her phone. "I texted my mom to see if she could watch my daughter, Angie, tonight while I work late here, but I forgot that Angie has a dance tonight that I was going to take her to." She sucks in a deep breath and takes in the room. "She's already upset because it's a father-daughter dance and the *father* part has been missing her whole life. I convinced her that I could go in place of her dad, but now I can't even do that." She makes a face. "I mean, I guess I can finish sanding the floors today and then stain them tomorrow, but then I'm losing a whole day's work tomorrow. But I guess I could make it up on Saturday, although I promised Angie that we'd make cookies on Saturday…"

"Don't kill yourself over this house, Cam." Even though it sounds nice, I still want her to finish the house in time. I feel bad for her and her daughter, but I need things done at a certain time.

"I already told you, it's all a chain reaction. If I delay this, it delays everything else. I really just have this week and next week and then we need to start bringing in furniture and decorations for you for the holidays. I can't delay anymore." She groans. "Okay. Let me figure this out."

I watch as she paces the room, then brings the phone to her ear.

"Mom? It's me. I *completely* forgot about the dance tonight…. No, I don't want to cancel, obviously, but — Can't you go instead of me?" She sighs. "No, I know. I promised her I would. But I have to work. Tonight is the only night for me to get this done." Her shoulders slump. "Angie's going to hate me for making her miss this dance. She was just starting to get excited about it."

"I can take her." The words coming from my mouth surprise even me. The whole situation is unfortunate and I just can't picture Cameron's little girl missing out on a fun evening with her friends just because she has a single mom who is working extra hard to make things work for their family.

Cameron looks over at me with confusion, but continues talking to her mom. "No, I can't delay things here. We're on a tight deadline."

"I can take her to the dance," I say louder.

"Hold on, Mom." She covers the phone and turns to me. "Are you being serious? Angie hasn't even met you."

I shrug. "If you don't want me to take her, I understand, but I just thought it'd make it easier for everyone. Angie would have her night out with her friends and you could finish up work here."

Cameron chews on the inside of her lip for a while. She raises the phone to her ear again and says,

"Mom? How do you think Angie would do if Luke Branson took her tonight? Yes, the guy who hired me for this project." There's a pause as she listens. "That's true. I can run home long enough to help her get ready, but then I'd need to get back to the house to stain the floors. And I'll be home in time for when they get back." She nods and cracks a small smile. "True. That should work. Thanks Mom. Crisis averted."

"So?" I ask after she hangs up the phone.

"Are you sure you're ready for a middle school dance?"

"Is *anyone* ever ready for a middle school dance?"

Cameron cocks her head to the side. "True. Listen, this is not a done deal. What matters here is Angie. If she takes one look at you and says no, then the answer's no. We'll just have to make do with the time we have. Got it?"

I put up my hands in surrender. "Of course. I'm doing this for Angie anyway."

She narrows her eyes. "Why is that? You don't even know her."

"No, but I know you and I know how hard you're working. I'd hate to see Angie suffer just because you're running out of your limited resources to help you."

She studies me a moment longer, then takes in a deep breath again. "I live at 314 Elm Street. Be there, ready to go by five o'clock and don't be late."

EVEN THOUGH I am typically better dressed than Cameron on any given day, it's still very uncomfortable for me to show up in a suit at her doorstep. Especially considering that I'm here for her daughter and *not* for Cameron.

A middle-aged woman answers the door and smiles brightly at me when she sees me. "Oh! You must be Luke!" She ushers me in and then pulls me in for a hug. "Angie is *so excited* for this dance!"

I smile back and look around at the house. It's certainly old. A lot of woodwork and antique furniture, but all displayed in a very modern and livable way. Cameron's house feels comfortable.

"Cameron!" the woman trills as she leads me down the hall. "Your daughter's date is here!"

We pass by a living room with a wide-open fireplace and a beautiful Christmas tree in the corner. There's a couch in the center of the room and the TV sits above the fireplace. There's also a large wooden table behind the couch in the opposite corner from the TV.

But we walk by all of that and into the kitchen in the back, where a little girl is sitting at a barstool at the counter and Cameron stands behind her and braids her hair.

"Hey Luke." Cameron smiles at me when she sees

me. "Just finishing up." She nods to the woman, "You've already met my mother, Alice. And this is Angie."

"Your date," the little girl says.

"It's very nice to meet you." I step forward and shake her hand, pretending to be as formal as possible in order to make Angie feel special.

Cameron leans in close to her daughter's ear and stage-whispers, "What do you think? You want to give it a try? Or do you want to kick him to the curb and stay home?"

Angie laughs and turns to her mom. "I'll give everyone a shot once."

"Oh dear, I hope that's not true." Alice places a hand on her chest and laughs.

Cameron ties off the braid and then holds up a mirror for Angie. "What do you think? Are you ready for your dance debut?"

"It's so pretty, Mom!"

Cameron kisses the top of Angie's head. "I'm glad you like it. You look beautiful, darling."

Angie slides off the chair and cautiously steps toward me.

I crouch down to her level. "We're going to have fun tonight. I'll have to break out my dance moves. Maybe show those kids there a thing or two."

Angie giggles.

"What do you say I go out and warm up the car so you can say goodbye to your mom?" I offer. "I'll be back to come get you in two minutes."

She nods shyly.

Alice follows me to the door and mutters, "Thank you so much for doing this. Angie really is looking forward to this dance. I would've taken her, but I have dinner plans. And, of course, you know how Cameron has to work."

"It's not a problem. We'll have fun."

Out at the car, I fire it up, blast the heat, and get the radio playing the Christmas music at a nice, easy volume. Then I grab the flowers I picked up at the grocery store on the way over and head back toward the house.

Angie already has on her pink winter coat by the time I make it back inside.

I hand her the flowers. "These are for you."

Her eyes widen in surprise. "Really?" She turns to Cameron. "Mom! Look! Aren't they pretty?"

Cameron nods. "They're very pretty. Let me see them and I'll put them in water so they're still fresh when you get back."

Angie hands her mom the flowers and then wraps her arms around her in a tight hug. "Bye Mom!"

"Bye, sweetie. Have fun!"

As Angie steps outside, I exchange glances with both Cameron and Alice. Cameron mouths a *thank you* and then turns back into the house.

Out at the car, I hold the door open for Angie and then go around to the other side to make the short drive to the school.

"Is everything to your liking?" I ask as I pull on my seatbelt.

"Yeah."

There's a noticeable shift in her demeanor, but I can't blame her. She just left her mom and her grandmother to go to a dance with a stranger. Naturally the girl is feeling a little shy.

I let the silence between us linger and allow the Christmas music to fill the space. Bing Crosby croons about a white Christmas.

"Are you going to date my mom?" Angie asks abruptly.

"Uh—well—why would you say that?"

She shrugs. "I just have a feeling that she likes you. And you must like her if you're taking me to this dance."

"Maybe I just like you."

She glances over at me. "You've never met me."

"Well…I…your mom works for me. That's all."

"Oh. Okay."

I turn onto East Avenue, grateful that the school is only around the corner. Once we get inside, this conversation will no longer be—

"It'd be okay with me," she goes on.

"What would?"

"If you dated my mom."

"Oh. Okay. You…you wouldn't be upset or anything?"

She shakes her head. "Grandma says Mom needs to get out more. And I think I agree. She's lonely. She says she isn't because she has me, but I think she is. And you seem nice. So why not?"

I grin and, to myself, I murmur, "Why not?"

"MOM!" ANGIE CALLS out throughout the house at the end of the night. "I'm home!"

"How was it?" Cameron stands at the end of the hall in the kitchen with her arms wide open to wrap her daughter in a hug.

"It was so much fun!" Angie says. "And Luke was really funny to watch dance."

"He was?" Cameron glances at me with a smirk.

"I can't say that 'funny' is what I was going for, but I'm glad you enjoyed it, Ange."

"I'm glad you had fun," Cameron says to Angie. "Hey, why don't you go upstairs and get in your pajamas and brush your teeth. If you want, you can pick out a story for us to read before you go to bed."

"Can Luke read it to me?"

Cameron looks to me. "If that's okay with him."

"Uh…sure!" I kick off my shoes by the door and step further inside.

Angie runs up the stairs toward her bedroom, leaving me and Cameron alone.

"Thanks again for taking her," Cameron says when Angie is out of earshot. "Sounds like you two had a good time."

"We did. It wasn't all that bad. Although, I did feel a little out of place being the only one without a kid."

"At least you were among other men. How do you think I feel in those situations?"

"True." I look around, both of us struggling for something to talk about now that our relationship has reached a more personal level. "So did you finish the floors?"

"Yep! I've actually been home for a little more than an hour. Just don't walk on them until I check them tomorrow."

"Wouldn't dream of it."

Our conversation dies off again and we stare away from each other, focusing on anything other than the other's face so that we don't have to acknowledge anything going on between us.

"I'm ready!" Angie calls from upstairs.

"Guess that's my cue," I tell Cameron. "Do you mind if I…?"

She waves me on. "No, go ahead. Her's is the first door on the left. Can't miss it."

Upstairs, it's obvious which room belongs to Angie. The walls are painted pink and there are a few stuffed animals in the corner, but also some posters of young male pop stars. The transitional room between girl and teenager.

Angie is snuggled in her bed and propped up against her pillow. *The Night Before Christmas* sits on her nightstand.

"Is this the book you want to read?"

She nods. "Uh huh. I know it's for little kids, but I love reading it this time of year."

I pull up a chair from her desk and take a seat beside her bed. "It's not a little kid book. I like it."

We only make it halfway through the book before Angie drifts off to sleep. I set the book on the nightstand again, reach over and turn out the light, and then proceed back downstairs.

Cameron is sitting at the table in the living room, working on a puzzle. "You're done already?"

I shrug. "She fell asleep."

She glances at the clock. "Wow. She must've worn herself out at that dance."

"She did have a lot of fun." I glance over at the puzzle. "How many pieces?"

"A thousand," she replies. "I thought it'd be a good idea, but now I'm kicking myself. I love puzzles, but I also love finishing things and this is definitely taking me much longer than I would like."

"Do you want some help?"

She studies me a moment, then smiles. "Sure.

Do you want something to drink? I've got a bottle of wine open."

"Nah, I'm okay. Thank you, though. Those middle schoolers sucked the energy out of me. If I had a drink, I think I'd fall asleep right here." I take a seat at the table beside her and start sorting through the pieces in the box. On the other side of the couch, the fire crackles in the fireplace. From somewhere behind Cameron, instrumental Christmas music plays.

"You have a great house," I tell her.

"Thank you. It didn't look like this when I bought it. This was going to be the start of my flipping business, but then I started to look into the history of it and I just couldn't do with a cheap flip. And then I was so invested in this house that it just made sense for me and Ange to move in. It's been home ever since."

"You restored all of this?"

She nods. "I told you. I know what I'm doing."

"I can see that." I take another look around. "Hopefully my house turns out as nice as this one. My folks will love it."

"I hope they do." Cameron takes a sip of wine and reaches for a puzzle piece.

"Your mom seems nice," I say after a second.

"Yeah."

I consider bringing up what Angie told me on the way to the dance, but decide against it. That was a private conversation between the two of us. Besides, if Cameron's not interested in me, I don't want to put either of us in an awkward situation. Especially when we have to continue to work together going forward.

"Do you have any siblings?" she asks me.

"I have a brother, who lives near my parents in Florida. But he probably isn't coming back for Christmas with them. He hates the snow."

"Still. He doesn't want to see you?"

"I go down there usually in January or February."

"That's not quite the same."

"No, it's not." I add a piece to the puzzle and then reach for another one. "What about you? Any siblings?"

Cameron shakes her head. "Nope. Just me. Luckily I have my parents, who live in town. But they're busy. Even though they're retired. They still help a lot with Angie, though."

"That's good."

"Yeah."

"And you're not…seeing anyone?"

She looks at me and her eyebrows raise. "No. I'm not. What about you?"

"No."

A playful smile spreads across her lips. "Is there a reason you're asking?"

I shrug. There's really no way to back out of this now. "I was just wondering if you wanted to go to dinner sometime. Just you and me. No moms. No kids. Maybe we could have a real conversation that isn't about work."

"And this isn't a real conversation?"

"It is. And I'm enjoying this. But I just thought— I don't know…"

"You're asking me out."

"Yes, I am."

She turns away and lets out a sigh.

"And you're turning me down."

"I never said no."

"And yet, you still haven't said yes."

"I'm nervous," she says. "I work for you."

"Sure, but you're not exactly my employee. After the job is done, if things don't work out with us, you could go your own way. Besides, I'm not asking you to marry me. I'm just asking you to dinner. Everybody eats."

"This is true."

"…So?" I push.

"You know what? Fine. What the hell?"

I chuckle. "Not exactly the enthusiasm I was looking for, but I'll take it. Does Friday at six work?"

Cameron makes a face. "I try to save Friday and Saturday nights for me and Angie since I'm usually working both jobs almost every weeknight."

"Both jobs?"

"I bartend at the brewery on Main Street."

"Oh, I didn't know that. That's cool. Okay. So

Friday is out. And if you're busy every weeknight, then maybe a…*lunch* date?" I cringe. "Oooh, this date just seems doomed from the start, doesn't it?"

She laughs. "I can make an exception to my weekend rule just this once. As long as it's okay with Angie. So this Saturday I can be free."

"Saturday? As in…tomorrow?"

She stares off as she thinks about it. "Oh jeez. Yeah, I guess so. Does that work for you?"

"Absolutely. I just hope my date from tonight doesn't get jealous."

DECEMBER 16TH
Cameron

❄ ❄ ❄

*I*m not sure exactly how to dress for my date with Luke. Could I even call it a *date*? I just spent the day baking with Angie and, up until my mother arrived to pick her up so I could get ready, I spent most of the day covered in flour and frosting.

Angie had no issue with me going on a date tonight instead of spending it in with her. In fact, she was even a little *too* enthusiastic that I go. That girl is growing up faster than I care for, being that she's already starting to think that her mom is uncool. Then again, I only have myself to blame for making her think that.

I debate what I should wear on the date. Usually, Luke sees me wearing clothes with holes in them or covered in plaster dust. Certainly not a representation of my "best self."

That's what I try to remind myself when I look in the mirror: *anything is better than the last time he saw you.* A good shower and some clean clothes go a long way.

In the end, I decide on black jeans and nice sweater. That way I'm comfortable and casual, but still dressy if the evening ends up calling for it.

The doorbell rings and I hurry down the stairs, careful not to trip in my new boots. They're dressy and girly and not something I typically wear, but it's nice to get dressed up every once in a while. I'm lucky that my job allows me to wear comfortable clothes that have been put through the ringer, but sometimes it's easy to get lost in all of that.

When I open the door, Luke is standing on the other side with a bouquet of flowers.

"Do you just have a stash of these for any emergencies?" I finish hooking in my earrings and take the bouquet from him. They smell amazing.

He laughs. "Not exactly the warm welcome I was hoping for, but I suppose it's better than some things you could've said."

I cringe. "Sorry. It's nice to see you. You look very handsome." I step aside. "Come in and I'll put these in water."

He steps inside and take another look at him. He really does look handsome. Under his black jacket he has a nice cream sweater with a red plaid button-up shirt on underneath. I look down and notice he's wearing jeans too, which helps me feel better about my own outfit.

He follows me down the hall toward the kitchen. "Where's Angie?"

"With my mom. They're both thrilled I'm going out tonight." I grab a vase from a cabinet in the breakfast nook and then carry it to the sink. "I don't know if that is an insult to my social life or what."

"A social life? What's that?"

I laugh as I start the tap. "Foreign concept, right?"

"Did you finish that puzzle?"

Luke had stayed until midnight last night, helping me work on the puzzle. We talked about everything—different jobs we've had, different people we've dated, who we knew in high school. Luke was three years younger than me and so we only tangentially knew each other's friends.

"No, I went to bed after you left. Haven't had time to work on it since and it's still too hard for Angie. Maybe we can work on it again after dinner."

Did I just invite my boss to stay the night? Then again, we're going on a date, so wouldn't that be a logical assumption? At least, depending on how well the night goes. So far so good, though…

"That sounds like fun."

I set the vase on the kitchen counter and we both exchange awkward smiles for a quick second before I blurt, "Ready?"

"The car's all warmed up for us."

He leads us outside. It isn't until I cut in front of him to open the door that I realize he was probably going to hold it open for me. Whoops.

"Sorry," I murmur. "Been a while since I've been on a date." *Should I have admitted that?*

Undeterred, Luke comes around to the other side of the car, gets behind the wheel, and pulls away from the curb.

"So where are you taking me for dinner?"

"Main Street Pizza," he says.

"Are we getting wings?" I joke. Even though I haven't been on a date in a while, even I know messy foods is not a good first date option.

"I was thinking wine and pasta. Have you been there to eat in the dining room?"

I shake my head. "No. When Angie was first born, she was a disaster to bring to restaurants and then when she settled down a bit, I was always so busy working that if we came to Main Street, it was just to pick up a pizza and take it home."

"Well then," he says with a smile. "You're in for a treat."

The drive is less than five minutes. One of the perks of living in town. Honestly, if it was the summer time, I would've suggested that we walked. But the wind whipping around the corner of the building before we get to the front door tells me that a walk would've been miserable and certainly not conducive to conversation.

Once we get seated at a table and the hostess finishes reading off the specials, I look around the dining room. The restaurant has taken over the neighboring storefront, leaving the brick wall between the two exposed. Against the brick wall, there's diamond-shaped wine rack that extends nearly up to the tall ceiling. Against the back wall, there's a lit-up sign with the restaurant's name that gives off an impression of elegance and charm.

"This is really nice. I've only ever seen it through the window," I say.

Luke looks around and nods. "They did a good job."

I turn my attention to the menu. "So what's good here?"

"It's all Italian food, so mostly pasta," he says. "But it's all delicious."

"It sounds delicious," I agree.

"Do you want to order some wine?"

"Like a bottle for the table? That's bougie."

He laughs. "It's a special night."

"Then sure."

We're both quiet as we survey the menu. By the time we each close our menus, having made our selections, we both sit in silence.

The waitress comes over and takes our orders, which breaks up the quiet that has become uncomfortable in the passing minutes. When she leaves, and conversation doesn't immediately strike up between us, I decide to break the silence myself.

"Are we being insane here?"

Luke furrows his brow. "Did you want to split a meal? I could call the waitress back…"

"No, not that! I'm talking about you and me. Should we be out on a date right now?"

"Why not?"

"How about just 'why'?"

He narrows his eyes. "I don't understand what you mean. Why is it so weird that we're on a date?"

"Maybe because we work together? Maybe because we've only known each other a couple weeks? Maybe because you took my daughter on a date before me?"

He smirks. "Are you feeling like sloppy seconds?"

"I'm being serious here, Luke. I mean, read the room. This is awkward."

"Only because you're making it awkward," he counters. "Last night when we were doing that puzzle, we had no issue with conversation."

"Maybe that was just a fluke." *Maybe that was the wine*, I add to myself.

"You want to know what I think?"

"Do I?"

He shakes his head. "I don't think you do."

That irritates me. "Just tell me."

Leaning back in his chair, he says, "You can't handle it."

"Tell me."

"No."

"Luke."

"Cameron."

I heave out a heavy sigh. "You're annoying."

"And you're not? Do you remember the first time we met when you came to see the house and you were listing all the things you were going to do and you expected me to take your word for it?"

"Well, you are, aren't you?"

"Only because you're so persistent."

"That's because—"

He holds up a finger to stop me. "You see what we're doing? We're having a conversation."

I roll my eyes. "This is hardly a good conversation for a date."

"Well, it's certainly better than the silence."

"So you *do* have a problem with the silence."

He shakes his head again. "No. You do. I was simply pointing it out. Now, are you ready to hear what I think?"

I look away, trying to feign disinterest. "As if you're even going to tell me."

"I think you've been burned by men in the past and so you've isolated yourself from any personal social interaction by piling on work and responsibilities with being a mother so that you can shelter yourself from the world. And now that we've found a way around that, you're getting cold feet because you're scared of getting hurt and I'm just not having it."

I study him for a few seconds. "You think you have me all figured out, don't you?"

"Not all. Just some. Honestly, it's the same problem I've had with contractors. And you broke through that barrier."

"And you're hoping to break through my barrier?"

He chuckles and reaches for his glass. "Well, we'll just see where the night takes us."

I blush and look away. "You're annoying."

"You've said that."

And I can't help but smile at him. Yes, things were initially awkward, but was that just me in my own head? Was I simply standing in my own way? Luke has called us both out for our behaviors and made it easier for us to have a conversation that it removed any sense of awkwardness.

Well played, Lucas Branson.

The rest of dinner passes with relative ease. Luke and I fall into easy conversation about the house. At first, I was hesitant to "work talk," but then Luke told me more about what he actually wanted to do with the house. How he wanted the other rooms to look. His plans for converting the apartment he currently lived in back into the second floor of a single-family house. How he hoped the house would be the center point for his family and the traditions they used to have. It all sounded very inspiring and sweet.

After Luke pays for the bill, we make our way back onto the street. It's still early and I actually don't want the date to end, but I don't know what else we'd do. I think it's still a little too soon to take him back to my house. The time would make the encounter awkward again. Either that or there'd be pressure to do more than I'm ready for. But the idea of working on the puzzle again with him sounds nice, so maybe we could do that instead.

"Interested in coffee?" he asks once we're outside.

"Oh, sure!" I smile and am grateful for the suggestion as the wind whips across my face.

Luke leads me down Main Street as we both brace against the weather. The closest coffee shop is on Jackson Street, which is two streets over from the restaurant.

By the time we make it inside, I know my cheeks are all rosy from the cold and only hope that it adds to my color instead of making me look like I'm sick.

Luke doesn't seem to notice. He steps right to the counter and orders his drink, then turns to me for my order.

I glance over the monthly specials — each with a holiday theme — and then order a hot macchiato. As if I'd ever consider an iced beverage on a frigid night like this.

"No problem," the barista says.

"Do you want to grab those seats over there by the window?" Luke asks.

There are a few people in here. One person writing at his computer at the bar top near the one window. Another person reading on the couch in the center of the room. There's a small group around the corner at the large dining table. Looks like they're playing some sort of card game.

"Sure, that looks cozy." I lead him over and take a seat in the plush leather seat. "Do you come here often?"

He shrugs. "Often enough. I try to stay local with everything, especially my coffee."

I nod. "So do I, but I have to admit that I don't make it here as often as I would like. Between work and Angie and…everything."

"You stop at Dunkin' every morning."

"Not anymore."

He smirks. "True. I'm your supplier, as of late."

"And do you come here?"

"Here, or the place on Harvester."

"I like it there too."

"Me too."

"See? So I *do* come here more often I realize." I smile at him, but the conversation dies off afterwards. In the ensuing quiet, I feel the need to bring something up that's been on my mind for most of the evening. "I like working with you."

"Likewise."

My hands wrangle together and I avert all eye contact. "And I like…spending time with you."

"It's really that painful for you to admit that, isn't it?" He laughs.

"Well, it's not exactly easy!"

At the counter, the barista calls out our drinks.

"I'll leave you hanging in suspense while I go get those." Luke rises from his seat and goes to fetch our drinks.

I watch him leave for a second, but someone else catches my eye.

"Cameron?" Bryce calls to me when he comes into the shop.

"Bryce," I murmur and shoot up to my feet.

He steps toward me and plants a kiss on my cheek. "What are you doing here?"

"I-I-I'm on a—" I look around him, hoping that Luke hasn't see him kiss me. But I'm not that lucky. Luke is right behind Bryce with a drink in each hand and a pained expression on his face.

He saw everything.

DECEMBER 16TH
Luke

❅ ❅ ❅

"**L**uke…" Cameron says under her breath, but I'm already turning away.

"Oh, I'm sorry. Did I interrupt something?" the man asks, looking between the two of us. He looks much more like Cameron's type. More of a blue-collar, rough-around-the-edges kind of guy. The type who would very much like to get his hands dirty right alongside Cameron. The type who could take the workload off her shoulders every so often.

The type who is almost the complete opposite of me.

The man extends his hand toward me. "I'm Bryce. Cameron's boyfriend."

I raise my eyebrows.

"He's not—" Cameron steps between us and glares at

him before meeting my eyes. "He's *not* my boyfriend."

Bryce rolls his eyes. "Okay. *Ex*-boyfriend. Whatever." He turns back to Cameron and reaches for her hands. "I was hoping that we could talk."

She pushes him away. "Not now, Bryce."

I start to turn toward the door. This date is clearly over—if it ever really was a date to begin with.

"Luke, wait!" Cameron reaches for my hand, but I pull away before she can grab mine.

"Cam, honey, what's going on?" Bryce asks.

"We were in the middle of something," she snaps at him. Then, back at me, she says, "I'm so sorry. This isn't what it looks like. Let's just go back to my place and I can expl—"

"Go back to *your* place?" Bryce asks from behind her. His voice is growing loud and the quiet, calm atmosphere of the shop has certainly been squashed. "Cameron, take a look at him. His hair is perfect, his clothes look spotless—why are you even with him? You don't go for guys like this.."

Again, she looks back at him. "Would you just go away? How do you know what kind of guys I go for?"

Bryce shakes his head. "Because I know you, Cam. And I told you that I'd take care of you. That's a promise I'm not going to take back. The offer still stands. I still love you. And I know you love me."

That does it. I step toward the door.

She seems stunned and it takes her until I make

it to the door before she realizes that I'm leaving. She runs to catch up to me, tugging at my arm to keep me from leaving.

"Wait! Luke! Don't go!"

I shake my head. "Why should I stay? There's clearly more going on between the two of you than there is between the two of us."

"No, it's not like that. Bryce is just…"

I raise my eyebrows, demanding an end to that sentence. "Is just *what*?"

She looks back toward him, but doesn't say anything else.

"Exactly," I say. "And that's why I'm leaving."

"No, Luke, wait!"

But I don't listen. Within seconds, I'm back out into the cold, bracing myself against the wind as I march back to the car.

How could I be so stupid? Someone as beautiful and strong as Cameron obviously already has someone in her life. And even if she didn't, why would she go for someone like me? Someone who has never had a blister in their life. Someone who would use their wallet to show strength instead of their muscles.

I'm nothing like Bryce. And clearly, he's the one she wants to be with. Not me.

The best thing I can do is to go home and forget that I had ever envisioned any kind of future between me and Cameron.

DECEMBER 16TH
Cameron

❆ ❆ ❆

"Luke, wait!" I watch as he escapes out into the cold night, power-walking down the sidewalk to get as far away from me as he could.

"Finally." I feel Bryce's hands grab my shoulders from behind me. "I thought he'd never leave."

I shrug out of his grasp and whip around to face him. "Back off, Bryce! Can't you take a hint? I don't want to be with you. Things between us are over. I was literally on another date with someone else. We're finished."

Bryce huffs, not used to being told no. "We have a future together, Cameron. I know you know it." He gestures out the door. "You're just upset because someone got hurt."

Shaking my head before he finishes, I say, "No, we

don't. I broke up with you long before I ever met Luke. He had nothing to do with my decision that we will *never* have a future together." I step to my seat and grab my coat. "If you'll excuse me, I need to go see if I can chase down someone I *might* have a future with."

With my coat in hand, I breeze by Bryce on my way out the door. He tries to reach for me again, but I pull away, my hand balled into a fist. The glare on my face a warning.

Bryce puts up his hands and takes a step back, allowing me to leave.

The cold hits me harder than I thought it would, although my burning anger toward Bryce keeps me at bay until I'm able to swing my coat over my shoulders and zip it up.

I race around the corner toward the parking lot where Luke had parked, hoping that he would have decided to hear me out and wait for me.

No such luck.

Luke's car is nowhere in the small parking lot. I pace up and down the rows just to be sure. When I'm finally convinced that he's not here, I consider my options: call my mother for a ride or walk home myself.

I opt for a walk. Not only will my mother — and my daughter — give me sympathetic looks and expect me to explain what had happened before I've had a chance to fully process it myself, but in a way I feel like I deserve the cold walk home. After all, I should've set Bryce straight a long time ago. Thanks to me, Luke got hurt. I shouldn't be surprised if he never wants to talk to me again.

December 18th

IT'S DISAPPOINTING TO see that Luke isn't at the job site on Monday. I was counting on seeing him so that I could explain what had happened at the coffee shop the other night, but I'm also not that surprised that he's not here. He's probably embarrassed. Hurt. Confused.

Can't say that I blame him.

With no one to talk to, I dig in and get to work. The plaster dust is still all over from the previous day. So are the various plastic tarp that I hung in the doorways and over the vents to keep the dust from traveling. Nothing is perfect, so I'll need to do a deep clean later, but at least it's help keep the mess mostly contained.

I start my day like I start any other: surveying the work that's already been done and refreshing the punch list. I double check the fireplace and the work that's been done by the fireplace expert I brought in. I check on the wiring, making sure that everything's done correctly so I don't accidentally spark a fire or any other mishap. And, finally, I check the patchwork I've done to the plaster, testing its smoothness and marking the points that need to be sanded down more.

No sense in cleaning and then making a mess again. I grab the sandpaper and get started on the patches that need touching up. It doesn't create as much dust as before, but enough to have to clean up. The dust falls to the floor like snow.

The good thing about sanding is that it's relatively mindless work. Unfortunately, that means that my thoughts keep wandering to everything that happened last night. I shouldn't have stayed behind to talk to Bryce—to put him in his place. I should've chased after Luke and tried to explain. Or maybe I shouldn't have gone out with Luke in the first place. Or, in the same vein, I shouldn't have ever gone out with Bryce, either.

Should've. Could've. Would've.

What's done is done. Now I just need to live with the consequences.

Out the window, I notice Luke coming up the sidewalk with a package tucked under his arm. It must be one of the fixtures I had to order that was delivered to his apartment.

My heart races at the sight of him and I stop working to greet him at the door.

The look on his face when he walks in tells me

that he's still not pleased with me.

"Good morning!" I try to convey a calm, happy demeanor in an effort to boost his mood.

Luke sets the box on the floor, but doesn't immediately respond to me. He surveys the room with his hands on his hips.

I watch him for a little bit, then finally say, "Luke, I'm sorry about what happened last night. I didn't mean to—"

"This place is a mess."

That takes me by surprise. "Excuse me?"

"Christmas is less than a week away," he goes on. "You said you'd have this place ready by then. Those were the terms you agreed to when you took on this project. If you didn't think you'd be able to get it done in time, then you should've conveyed that to me at the start."

The attack on my work lights a fire in me. "I'm doing the best I can."

"Yeah, but you're not doing it fast enough."

"I'm almost done."

He waves his hands around the room. "What part of this looks 'almost done'? Sure, let me bring in the Christmas tree and the lights and—oh yeah!—the furniture. This is nowhere *near* ready!"

As if you would know, I think to myself, but hold that snipe back. "Luke, I promise you I'm going as fast as I can. Restorations take longer than flips."

"Not if you had listened to me."

"Oh? So you're the contractor now? Excuse me, but I think that *you're* the one who reached out to *me* and agreed to hire me on the spot. If you're such an expert, then do the job yourself!"

"I've flipped plenty of houses."

"And they all look the same," I snap. "You just suck the charm right out of them. Paint the trim white and the walls gray. Call it 'chic' and jack up the rent, and—boom—you're suddenly a flipper." I roll my eyes. "Please. What you really are is a slumlord."

"Are you saying my units are dirty?"

"I'm saying the landlord is. You're so intent on making a profit that you forget that what you're offering is a place where people live. But you're fixing houses, not building homes, so I wouldn't think you'd understand the time it takes to put into a restoration like this one. I'm sorry, but I thought that's what you wanted."

Luke clenches his jaw. "Maybe I'm rethinking what I wanted."

"Maybe you should."

"And maybe you shouldn't come to work tomorrow."

That breaks all of my resolve. "Are you firing me?"

Luke looks away, but doesn't respond to me.

The silence builds until I can't stand it anymore. I cross the room, grab my things, and storm out of the house.

December 19th
Luke

❄ ❄ ❄

Unsurprisingly, Cameron isn't at the house this morning. And why would she be? I explicitly told her not to come back. The memory of it makes me feel ashamed. Who does something like that right before Christmas?

Instead, I pace the dusty living room, lying to myself that I could finish it all up on my own. Of course I can't. I don't know the first thing about home renovation. I only know who to call. And Cameron made that abundantly clear yesterday when she rightfully called me out on it.

I let out a sigh after I come to the realization that I've hit rock bottom. This place is a mess. There's certainly no way that I'll be able to get it ready in time to spend the holidays here with my parents. Better to break the news now than to spring it on my folks when they arrive.

Mom picks up after the first ring. "Lucas? Good morning, my sweet boy!"

"Hi Mom."

"What's the matter? What's wrong?" Somehow, a mother always knows.

"Well…I'm afraid I have some bad news."

"Are you hurt? What happened? Tell me."

"No, Mom, nothing like that. It's just that…the house isn't going to be done by the time you come."

The panic vanishes from her voice. "Oh. We know that, honey. It's a big house and you're converting it back to a single family. Of course it's not going to be completely done in time for Christmas. You'd have to be a miracle worker to do that."

"That's just it. It's not going to—"

"Jim?" Mom calls to my dad away from the phone. "Lucas is on the phone. Come and say hi!" Then, back to me she says, "Honey, your father wants to talk to you. I'll put you on speaker."

I close my eyes as the conversation lulls. It takes a while for them to figure out how to put the phone on speaker. The two of them banter with one another on the other end.

"Is it this button? No, that one mutes it. Honey? Lucas, dear, can you hear us? Jim, why isn't he talking?"

"You haven't pressed anything yet, Harriett. Press that button."

"Is it a button if it's a touch screen?"

"Not that hard! You don't need to break the phone."

"It's impossible to tell. I hate these stupid smart phones."

"Luke, say something," Dad tells me. "Your mother doesn't believe me that you're on speaker."

"Can you hear me?" I ask.

"There we go!" Mom cheers.

"How's the weather up there?" Dad asks. "Snowing yet?"

"Yeah, we have snow," I say. "It's not too chilly—maybe in the low-thirties—but I'm sure you two will be freezing since you're Flordians now."

"I'm already all packed," Mom says. "Our flight leaves tomorrow evening. We're taking a redeye, so it'll be late by time we get there."

"Just text me the details," I say. "Look, I wanted to talk to you about—"

"How's the house?" Dad asks.

"Yes, that's what I've been trying to tell you. The house won't be done."

"Of course not," he says. "It's nearly two thousand square feet and over a hundred years old!"

"I don't think—"

"I'm so excited to see how it's coming along, though," Mom says. "Oh, I just remember all the Christmases we used to have there. I love it that you've bought it and are fixing it up. Just promise me you'll keep the woodwork and everything."

"Of course," I say. "Why wouldn't I?"

There's a noticeable silence on the other end. Then Dad says, "You just tend to paint over those kinds of details."

"Are you saying you don't like the houses I've done?" Every time I have a new listing, I always send a link to my parents so they can see the pictures. The texts back are short, but encouraging.

"Beautiful!"

"Nice!"

"Well done!"

Now I'm wondering what their true thoughts were behind those encouragements.

"Honey, we love how successful you are," Mom says.

"That's not exactly what I'm asking. Do you or don't you like my houses?" After another moment's pause, I add, "Be honest."

"Well…" Mom starts.

"You…have a certain, uh, *style* of doing things that we…"

I nod. Enough said. "So you don't like them."

"Hey, they're selling, so what do we know?" Dad asks. "Besides, we're the generation that covered up the hardwood floors, so we're equally to blame for bad design choices."

"Listen, honey, we have to run," Mom says. "I have a hair appointment in half an hour. I love you and I can't wait to see you. Your father will text you when we leave."

"Okay." I'm still stunned that they just admitted they didn't like my houses. "Have a safe trip. Love you too."

"Looking forward to seeing you, son," Dad adds.

"You too."

❄ ❄ ❄

HEARING THE ENTHUSIASM in my parents' voices about seeing the house helps motivate me to try to get this house done in time. Now I only need Cameron on board, which means I need to apologize for the things I've said and actually hear her side of the story.

As uncomfortable as that will be.

When Cameron's not working as a contractor, I know she works at the brewery on Main Street, so I head there. There isn't a hostess as the station when I first walk in, so I scan the room.

Being that it's the middle of the afternoon, it's not too busy, so I can survey the workers pretty quickly. Unfortunately, I don't see Cameron anywhere.

"Bar or table?"

I'm snapped out of my own head. "Hmm?"

The hostess has returned to the station. "Are you waiting for anyone else or…?"

Or are you eating alone? The end of her sentence goes unfinished, but it's so poignant that it still can't be ignored.

"Um…just me," I say. "The bar is fine."

She smiles. "You can take any seat you'd like. Someone will be right with you."

"Thanks," I murmur, then head over to the bar. I've really only been here at night when it's jam-packed full of people, which is nice to see, but having the place quiet is also a nice alternative.

I survey the menu, but am interrupted by the bartender.

"Have we decided yet?"

Based on the name tag on her shirt, her name is Laurel.

"I guess I'll get the number two and…maybe some pretzels." I don't have the food menu in front of me, but I had them the last time I was here and they were pretty good. Plus, if I'm going to drink in the middle of the day, I need to have something else in my stomach.

"Sure thing." She reaches for a glass under the bar and turns to fill it at the tap.

"Cameron isn't working, is she?"

When Laurel turns around, she raises her eyebrows. "Who's asking?"

"Um, I'm…a friend." Is that what we are?

Laurel sets the glass in front of me. "She called in. Had to go pick up her daughter from school. Guess she has a stomach ache. Too much junk food the last week of school before break."

I make a face as I think of sweet Angie not feeling well. "I'm sorry to hear that."

"Me too." Laurel studies me. "Are you the guy who fired her?"

"I didn't—" I start, then concede, "Yeah, I guess I am."

"That's a shame that you had to go and do that," Laurel says with an edge to her voice. "Cameron loved working on that house. She would come in here every day yapping on about it."

"She did?"

"Oh yeah. She even said it was great to work for such an understanding and caring guy who gave her the freedom to do what needed to be done to the house."

That stings.

"Guess she misjudged you," Laurel adds.

"That's not exactly what happened. We had a fight. I was hoping to talk to her about it."

Laurel fills another glass at the tap, then takes it to someone down the bar. When she comes back, she says, "You're going to have to do something really big to make it up to her. You really hurt her. She liked you a lot."

"She did?"

"Are you telling me you didn't like her the same way?" Laurel has her hand on her hip and looks at me down her nose. "Aren't you the one who brought her coffee every day? Who visited the job site more often than most homeowners?"

I let out a sigh, then nod. "Yeah. I guess I like her too." It feels good to admit it. "I like her a lot, actually."

"So then why did you have to go and break her heart like that?"

"I didn't mean to break her heart, but when her boyfriend crashes our date —"

"Boyfriend?" Laurel cuts in. "Cameron doesn't have a boyfriend."

"Bryce?"

She waves it off. "He's not her boyfriend."

"Then why did he kiss her?"

"They used to date, but they were never a good fit. He has a good job and lots of money and she got swept up in all of that for a moment." Laurel takes a rag and starts wiping the top of the bar. "Honestly, I think she was thinking about Angie the whole time." She looks up at me. "You know who Angie is, right?"

"Yeah, I do." I nod. "Took her on a date before Cameron."

Laurel smirks. "Good man. Anyway, things between Cameron and Bryce fell apart because he thought he could buy his way to her heart. But when Cameron broke up with him, it was the first time someone had ever told him no. It didn't matter how much money he had or the gifts he bought her. He wasn't a good fit for her and her family."

"So where do things stand between them now?" I ask quietly.

"There's nothing there," Laurel says. "They broke up over a year ago, but he just won't face facts. He may be chasing her, but she will not go back to him. I swear, on my life, that she's completely single. She was even interested in you, until…"

Until I went and blew it.

DECEMBER 19TH
Cameron

❄ ❄ ❄

The doorbell rings and I have to extricate myself from my place on the couch beside Angie, who has fallen asleep in front of the TV. We're in the middle of *Elf*, which I've seen a million times, but it's Angie's favorite so I let her watch it over and over again.

When I answer the door, I almost immediately slam it shut, but the kindness my mother instilled in me prevails.

"What do you want?" I demand.

Bryce puts up his hands in surrender. "Hey, take it easy! I just came here to talk."

I glance back into the living room, where Angie is still asleep, then turn back to Bryce. "Well, I can't talk right now. Angie's not feeling good. We were going to watch movies for the rest of the day."

He pushes past me to look into the living room himself. "Seems to me like she's asleep. You have time to talk." He steps in and closes the door behind him.

"Look, you can't stay long," I say in a hushed voice. "Angie needs me."

"She's sleeping."

"Not for long. She comes first. Above all else. And everyone else."

He rolls his eyes. "Yes, Cam. I've heard the lecture before."

"I wouldn't have to lecture you if you actually showed an interest in her."

"I show interest in her."

"Every date you've suggested, it was always just the two of us. Never her."

He scoffs. "That's because I'm dating *you*. Not your daughter."

And that seals the deal. Never again will I ever consider the possibility of mine and Bryce's romantic future. There isn't one. From Day One, he has proved that he doesn't care about Angie. Not like Luke does.

"You're wrong. I have a kid, so when you date me, my daughter is part of the deal. If you can't accept that and welcome her, then I have no time for you." I place my hand on his shoulder and start to lead him back toward the door.

Bryce pushes away my hands. "Wait a minute.

Wait a minute! I can accept the fact that you have a daughter."

"Right, but you won't include her in anything."

"You want me to include her? I'll take her to the zoo next week."

I shake my head. "It's too late. We're done. To quote the great Taylor Swift, we are never ever getting back together." That was a little more sarcastic than was probably necessary, but I'm getting tired of saying the same thing over and over to him.

"Cameron, wait. Let's talk about this."

"No, Bryce. There's nothing to talk about." I open the door and step back to allow him to exit. "Please leave me alone. The two of us are never going to happen."

"I'll take care of you. Anything you could ever want, I'll buy it for you."

I shake my head, glad that he finally found his way outside again. "What I need money can't buy."

And with that, I shut the door and lock it with a sense of finality that makes me feel good right down in my soul.

❄ ❄ ❄

THE CLASSIC CLAYMATION of *Rudolph the Red-Nosed Reindeer* finishes up when the doorbell rings again. It's been hours since Angie and I had been interrupted, so I decide to get up and get the door.

On the other side stands Luke.

"Hey," he says.

I give him a shy smirk. "Hey."

"Mind if I come in?"

"Sure." I step aside and let him in, closing the door behind him.

"Luke!" Angie races in from the living room and reaches for his hand. "What are you doing here?"

He kneels down to her level. "Well, I heard you weren't feeling well and I just wanted to see how you were doing."

My chest burns with delight at how much he's taken an interest in her. I'm sure she's not the reason he's here, but the way he makes her feel so special warms my heart.

"I feel much better," she says. "Mom and I watched movies all day."

"Oh yeah? Any good ones?"

"Just Christmas movies," she says. "We watch them every year, but this year Mom's been so busy working that we haven't had a chance to watch a lot of them."

He makes a face. "I think that's partly my fault."

"That's okay. She likes working for you."

"Okay!" I blurt. This conversation is getting too personal. "Angie, it's getting late. You still need to go up and take a shower before bed."

Angie rolls her eyes. "Fine, Mom." Her demeanor softens when she turns back to Luke. "Thanks for coming. I wish you could stay longer. Mom says you're good at puzzles. I'd love to do one with you."

"I think that can be arranged," he says. "But I think you should listen to your mom right now. She and I need to talk."

Angie turns toward the stairs.

"I'll be up soon," I tell her as she stomps up each step.

Luke and I are both quiet until we hear the water running.

"I'm sorry—" I start, but the sound of Luke's voice stops me.

"No, it's my fault."

"It's just that Bryce took me by surprise at the coffee shop and he and I had this history and…" I trail off and meet his eyes. "Sorry."

He shakes his head. "Don't be. I should've let you explain. I overreacted and the whole thing was my fault." He reaches for my hand. "I'd like to rehire you, if you're interested."

I can't help but smile at that. "Of course. You didn't hire some sloppy contractor in my place, did you?"

"Wouldn't dream of it."

I smile again, but drop my head and murmur, "I'm sorry about what I said about you. I don't think you're a slumlord, and I don't think you're bad at your job. I just think you focus too much on the numbers and less on the home."

He nods. "I know. You're right. I'm learning."

With a deep breath, I ask, "So…is that it?"

Luke studies me for a moment. Next thing I know, his lips are on mine.

When he pulls away, he says, "I'd like to see you more than just working on the house."

"Bryce didn't scare you away?"

He rocks his head back and forth. "Laurel told me the story between you two."

"Did she now?"

"And she gave me hell for making you feel bad. I'm sorry."

"I think we've already said all that."

"You're right," he says. "No more sorrys between us."

I laugh. "Right, because there is no place for sorrys in a relationship."

He chuckles at that one too. *Of course* there will be more sorrys. Just…hopefully not for a while.

"So is it really over between you and him?" Luke asks shyly.

"Yes. Definitely. He came by this afternoon to try to win me back, but he showed just how much of a jerk he really is. And how much he doesn't value Angie." I shake my head. "No amount of money can make up for disrespecting my daughter."

"Of course not."

"The truth is, he viewed her as a nuisance and not a special part of my life."

Luke smiles. "I think Angie's great. And, actually, one of the things I admire most about you is how much you put her above everything else. You're a mother, first and foremost. And I respect that a lot."

I step toward him and wrap my arms around him, laying my head on his chest. His hug feels warm. Comfortable. Safe.

"That's why I like you," I tell him. "You don't want to change me."

CHRISTMAS EVE
Luke

* * *

"Oh, honey!" Mom cheers when she steps through on Christmas Eve. "This is *beautiful*!"

I smile wide as I step in behind her and Dad. Cameron and Angie trail behind us too.

Cameron really did pull it off, so I couldn't leave her out of the big reveal. The living room looks gorgeous. As long as you can look past the ruggedness of the neighboring rooms. Which isn't hard to do with the giant Christmas tree in the window and the garland and wreaths adorned in a very sophisticated way. Apparently Cameron also has an eye for design.

"You like it?" I ask.

"This is amazing," Dad says.

Mom dabs tears away from her eyes and presses a

hand to her chest. Finally, she chokes out, "It really is so nice."

"I'm glad you both like it."

Dad looks around me at Cameron, who is still lingering in the doorway with Angie. "And you did all the work?"

She shrugs. "Most of it, yeah."

He shakes his head as he looks around again. "Beautiful."

"The rest of the house is still unfinished," she explains. "We'll get to that after the holidays, but Luke told me how much the two of you were looking forward to spending Christmas here."

Mom nods. "I remember spending many Christmases here. Funny how being in a space brings back so many memories I thought I had forgotten." She walks over to the fireplace, where there's a fire roaring in the hearth. "My sisters and I would fight over the order the stockings were hung. My mom tried to insist that it was in birth order, but we would always switch them around." She looks over to where the tree is in the window. "And that's where we'd always have the tree, to light up not only our house but the whole neighborhood. Seeing it as I walked up..." She breathes in a deep breath. "Well, it was really special."

I look over at Cameron and smile, then silently mouth a "thank you."

"You remember when the tree fell down on

Christmas Eve, right before the whole family came over?" Dad asks.

Mom rolls her eyes, but smiles. "Oh, I've never been so embarrassed and frustrated at the same time! That was a *mess*!" She looks to Cameron. "I'm sure Luke told you about that. That was the one year we tried a real tree. The whole damn thing came crashing down and I said forget it. We've done an artificial tree ever since."

Cameron smiles politely. "Yeah, Luke did mention that."

I give her an *I told you so* look.

Mom seems to get wrapped up in the house again, as she looks up and down at every intricate detail that Cameron has worked on for the last couple weeks.

To my surprise, she walks over to Cameron and wraps her in a hug. "Thank you for giving me these memories back. You did a beautiful job. It all looks just like it did when I was a little girl."

When she pulls away, Cameron smiles and nods. "Of course. I always try to keep the spirit of the home alive with each of my restorations. This one isn't finished yet, but it's on its way."

Mom looks around. "I'm looking forward to seeing the final thing."

"Me too," I say. "She does good work. And she keeps me in line."

"Now *there's* a job," Dad adds, and we all laugh.

"Did this little girl help you too?" Mom asks,

leaning down toward Angie.

"Mom and I went to the hardware store a lot," Angie says. "After school."

Cameron laughs. "Sometimes that's the only chance I had."

"Are you going to grow up to be a contractor like your mom?" Mom asks.

Angie makes a face. "No. She's always dirty."

Everyone laughs again.

"Thanks, Ange," Cameron says with a smirk.

We're quiet as my parents walk around the room. Mom is still misty-eyed and Dad examines the woodwork, which has all been sanded down and varnished to give it a good polish.

"Well, should we go up to the apartment and get the gifts?" Dad asks. "I'd love to have a good family Christmas down here in our old family home."

"That sounds like a great idea!" Mom cheers. "Oh, I'm so excited to have family in this house again!"

"We'll let you guys have your family Christmas—" Cameron starts to say, but Mom waves a hand at her.

"Honey, you gave us our home back. You're family. Stay and celebrate with us—the both of you. Unless you have other plans?"

I watch as Cameron considers it. She looks down at Angie and asks, "What do you think?"

"I think I want to stay here!" Angie says. Then, to

my surprise, she comes over and takes my hand. "With Luke."

Mom clutches her chest again. "Oh, how sweet!"

"Are you sure?" I ask Cameron. "I don't want to leave anyone hanging if you have plans."

"We can stay for a while," she tells me. "Mom won't be over until tonight so Angie and I have nowhere to be until then."

"Good!" Dad says. "I'll go start bringing down the gifts."

After he leaves, I start to follow him out, but the way Mom's looking at Cameron stops me. She reaches for her hand and says, "I'm so glad you two are staying to celebrate with us. I can tell that you're the special girl in my son's life."

Cameron blushes and looks down.

Mom turns to me. "Don't you let this one go!"

I can't help but smile. "I wouldn't dream of it."

ACKNOWLEDGMENTS

This project would not have been possible without the support of my Kickstarter backers! Thank you all for your support!

Lisa Renee

Anna L

Elise Faber

AA Briggs

John Idlor

Ruthenia (RAD)

Stephanie Wollman

Heiko Koenig

Gary Phillips

Anonymous Reader

A chance moment. A snow storm. And the gift of a new beginning.

Tristan is ready to party and ring in the New Year by kissing his soon-to-be girlfriend, Julie. The only bad note in his rocking night is the ongoing snow storm. Outside his apartment, he's almost hit by a swerving car! Behind the wheel is Grace, the most beautiful woman with haunting green eyes. She's on her own mission to get home to her grandfather.

In a selfless act reminiscent of the age of knights and chivalry, Tristan vows to get her home…never realizing they are both on a date with destiny and their lives will be forever changed by the SNOW AFTER CHRISTMAS…

More by the Author

To find more books by the author, visit
DavidNethBooks.com/Books

* * *

Subscribe to his newsletter to be the first to know of new
releases and special deals!
DavidNethBooks.com/Newsletter

* * *

If you enjoyed the book, please consider leaving a review
on Goodreads or the retailer you bought it from. Reviews
help potential readers determine whether they'll enjoy a
book, so any comments on what you thought of the story
would be very helpful!

About the Author

D. Allen is the author of the sweet small town romance series, Montana Beach and Small Town Christmas.

Also writes fantasy and superhero fiction as David Neth.

www.DavidNethBooks.com
www.facebook.com/DavidNethBooks

www.ingramcontent.com/pod-product-compliance
Lightning Source LLC
Chambersburg PA
CBHW030807190726
48285CB00003B/1062

She scoffs. "Not all of us can buy up rental properties on a whim. I *need* this job."

I consider telling her the truth: that the only reason I'm in a position to buy a rental property is from my grandfather's life insurance. I thought it would be a good way to honor him, by giving the rental a fishing theme. It was something he loved to do.

But no. If Steph is going to snap at me like that and take personal jabs, then she doesn't deserve to know the truth. Just a few days ago, we were perfect strangers. In two weeks' time, we probably will be again. Whatever I thought was between us apparently never existed in the first place.

Steph drops her toast back on her plate and wipes her hands in a napkin. "You know what? You're right. I shouldn't even be on vacation when my job is on the line. I need to get home."

I consider asking her to stay. I consider telling her that the radio said there's going to be some nasty weather coming this afternoon. I consider a lot of things.

But I don't speak up on any of them.

Instead, I watch as she disappears into her bedroom to pack up her things.

DECEMBER 21ST
Carson

❄ ❄ ❄

The radio was right. A big storm is on the horizon. Stung from Steph actually leaving, I venture out to Main Street, too stubborn to admit that it's probably a bad idea with the impending snowstorm. I just need to get out of the house. I can't sit there, on the couch, where less than twenty-four hours earlier I thought something was sparking between me and Steph, only to have it completely fizzle out by breakfast.

I make it to a boutique on Main Street that sells home goods. I browse the knickknacks, not shopping for anything in particular.

Along the back wall are Christmas ornaments. That's the one thing that's lacking from the tree Steph and I got together for the house: Ornaments. We have the lights and the popcorn, and I managed to find some tinsel in the garage, but there aren't any ornaments on the tree at all.

The display is filled with unique ornaments. These aren't the ones you'd find on grandma's traditional tree with hand-painted ceramics. These are cheap glittery ones that are probably way overpriced for what it costs to make them.

Okay. I'm being bitter.

My eyes land on one in particular. A peanut butter and jelly sandwich, encrusted around the outside in golden glitter. Instantly, it reminds me of Steph and I grab it. I can be bitter and miss her at the same time, right?

As I step up to the register, the bell above the door rings as someone else walks in. I glance up only briefly and see that it's Daisy from the food drive at the church.

Immediately she recognizes me. "Oh hi! How are you?"

I smile. "Good. You?"

"Just doing some last-minute shopping."

Nodding I say, "Yeah, I guess I am too."

"Where's your—" She wiggles her finger beside me. "—your, uh, friend. What was her name? Steph?"

"She needed to head back home earlier than she thought."

Daisy pouts her bottom lip and drops her

shoulders low. "Oh bummer! You two were so cute together!"

"But we're not—"

She adjusts her purse strap on her shoulder. "You're not a couple. So you said. But I'm not dummy and I could tell there was something between you two." She sticks her hip out and puts a hand to it, hooking an eyebrow in my direction. "Look me in the eyes and tell me you don't feel something special for that girl."

Turning back to the shopkeeper, I take my card back. "It doesn't matter now," I say to Daisy. "Steph's gone. We won't see each other ever again."

She drops the pose and rolls her eyes. "You two were complete strangers before you met, right? Both from different cities?"

I shrug an acknowledgement.

"That's fate!" she nearly shouts in a nasally voice. "You two met for a reason. You can't just let a sign from the universe like that slip away without doing something about it."

"But she's gone."

"So go after her," Daisy says. "You'll regret it if you don't." She pats my shoulder as she walks by, leaving her words to linger in the air in her absence.

Five minutes later, I'm climbing back in my car and pulling out onto the snow-covered street.

The storm has certainly arrived.

The short drive back to the house is tough, even

in my four-wheel drive. The trouble is that I can't see much with how much it's snowing. Add in the dusk hour, the unfamiliar streets, and it's a wonder I make it back to the house at all.

Climbing out of the car, I consider shoveling, but brush it aside. With as much as it's snowing, it would be pointless. Sooner and later I'm going to have to face the music: I'm alone in this big ol' house.

Isn't that the vacation that I first signed up for? If I had known that I would feel this lonely, I would have just stayed home.

December 21st
Steph

* * *

The weather is terrible. My little sedan can hardly maneuver in all the slushy snow on the road, and the angle that the snow is falling is making it impossible to see much of anything. Luckily, there's someone in front of me to follow, because otherwise I would have no idea where I was on the road.

I do know this much: I haven't made it far outside of Batavia. My plan was to take Clinton Street all the way out to Bergen and take the 490 back to Rochester. But I haven't even made it to Bergen yet and I have no idea how far away it is. My surroundings are shrouded in snow.

The time alone has left me time to think, for better or for worse. I'm a big enough person to admit that I may have overreacted to that email I got this morning. Stupid Richard told Monica that he found the stupid plans. She had emailed me to tell me "not to worry" about it.

Bull.

I've worked there long enough to know that as soon as I come back from this impromptu vacation, she's going to expect an explanation out of me. And she's going to judge every one of my responses harshly. She values actions, not words.

Richard, meanwhile, is at the office while I'm not. He's spinning whatever story suits him because I'm not there to say anything to the contrary. Monica, for all of her business savvy, isn't so great with people. She's gullible. She'll believe whatever story Richard tells her and take it as the gospel truth.

Which means that I will likely be out of a job by the time I get back.

Knowing Richard, he'll take whatever changes I've made to the Kellogg account—which I did all on my own—and claim them as his own in the final draft. He'll probably tell Monica that I didn't help at all. And she'll believe him.

That's why I need to get back so I can set the story straight. Clear my name. Call Richard out for his lies. Take ownership of the work that's rightfully mine.

An oncoming car passes in the next lane and I grip the wheel tighter. I hate it when that happens. I hate driving at night in general, but especially in this weather. It's too snowy. I can't see the road. I don't know the twists and turns out here. I just want this trip to be over.

My mind goes to Carson and the big, beautiful house I'm leaving him behind in. Even though the trip had a bumpy start and was cut short, it was a lot of fun. Carson made it that way. The whole situation could've turned out very awkward awkward, but the two of us clicked. It was…surprising. A sweet surprise.

And now, to think I've left him all alone back at the house. I don't like it. I wish I could've stayed. But I need to make sure I have my job.

We were getting too close anyway. I mean, I've only known him a couple days and yesterday I was practically sitting in his lap. Technically, it was *laying*, but still. That's not me. That's not what I do or how I act. So why is Carson different? What is it about him that makes me act differently?

Needing a distraction, I reach over and turn up the radio. Snoopy's piano solo plays and I let myself focus on the music and on the road.

The brake lights on the car in front of me suddenly glow red and I immediately lift my foot off the gas, feeling the car start to slow. My foot hovers over the brake, ready to stomp on it in case I need to. It's a habit that I need to consciously tell myself not to give in to. Hitting the brakes would make me slide—probably into a ditch—and that would only make this day worse.

The car ahead pulls into a driveway that I only see when their headlights shine on the reflectors lining the path under the mound of snow.

After the car is gone, I press the gas slowly and forge on…alone.

There's no one behind me or in front of me and it takes even more concentration to focus on staying on the road and not drifting off. There are faint tire tracks that I make sure to stay within as best I can. I end up turning down the radio a bit to cut out any unnecessary distractions. My whole body is tense with stress.

Up ahead, I cross an intersection where the tire tracks I'm following turns to the right. I keep on going straight, forging a new path in the snow with my little car. I picture the grill pushing the snow in front like a snow plow and my mind wanders to worse thoughts. The car overheating and shutting off. Or worse, starting on fire.

My nerves are getting the better of me, but I keep my hands locked on the steering wheel and do my best to follow the road, which winds up along a small hill. One that's apparently too much for my car to get any momentum in with the snow.

Tires spin as I slow to a stop. I look in my rearview mirror and am glad that no one is behind me. I shift into reverse, feel my car slide back down the hill, then shift into drive to try to take the hill at a higher speed. Only, when I press the gas, my tires just spin while my car stays in place.

"Shoot," I mutter. "Shoot shoot shoot."

Must be a patch of ice or something under the snow. I shift into reverse again and move back, angling my car off the road a bit. But when I shift into drive again, my tires still just spin. Trying reverse for the third time has the same results.

I'm stuck.

"Shoot!" I shout.

Hitting my four-way lights, I put the car in park and open the door to survey the damage. Maybe I can dig out around the tires, give the car some room to get some friction on the roadway.

When I open the door, though, I can already tell what the problem is. The snow is too high. With the swing of my door, I also push aside a couple inches of snow.

I start to get out, but think better of it. In the car I'm protected. From the elements, from any oncoming traffic. The best thing to do is to admit defeat and call someone.

The problem is, I have no idea where I am. Somewhere between Batavia and Bergen. Nobody I know in Rochester is going to brave this storm to come and get me. It's too far of a drive.

There's only one person I can call for help.

DECEMBER 21ST
Carson

Steph greets me out in the snowy roadway when I pull up behind her. My four-wheel-drive has made the excursion here with only a little difficulty, but even then, I could feel the tires pulling.

"Sorry," she says over the wind. "Thanks for coming out to get me. I don't know what happened! My car just couldn't make it up the hill."

I motion to the back end of her vehicle. "I can tell you why you're stuck right now. The back end of your car is halfway in the ditch."

"Oh."

Returning to my car, I pull a shovel out of the back and return to her car.

"What are you doing?" she asks.

"Well, we have to get your car back on the road," I explain as I start digging into the snow around her tires. "If not, then you're not getting this out until the spring when the snow thaws. It'll only take a couple snowplows to go by to bury the whole thing and then it'll be impossible to move in the packed snow."

"Oh," she says again. "Is there anything I can do to help?"

"Not right now." I'm being short with her, but I can't help but feel annoyed. If she wasn't giving me the cold shoulder this morning, maybe I could've talked her into staying and then we wouldn't be out here on the side of the road in the cold and snow. But I keep all of this to myself and work in silence.

Steph obviously wants to say something, but she doesn't. Instead, she stands by and watches as I dig out the back end of her car as best I can in the storm.

I clear out the snow all around her car too, not even attempting to get the snow underneath. It would obviously be ideal to have it out, but my fear is that I'll pack it too much and then ruin the mechanicals underneath. Or worse, the packed snow would act as if the car were sitting on top of a rock.

"Okay, get in and put it in drive," I tell her. "But don't get crazy with it! You only want to move up a few feet. Make sure to turn the wheel so you can pull back onto the road."

"Do you just want to do it?" she asks.

"And you're going to stand back here and help

push the car out?" I snap. "No, you do it."

Without another word, she slides back behind the wheel and shifts into gear. Shortly after, the engine revs and the wheels spin. The car rocks a little, fishtailing back and forth.

Pressing my hands against the back of the car, I use all of my strength to try and help push it out of the cradle its sunk into. The tires continue to spin, but it shifts enough that it looks like it's at least on the pavement and not on the shoulder of the road.

Tapping the top of the trunk, I yell out, "That's enough!"

Steph cuts the engine and gets out of the car. "You think it'll be okay here?"

"Put a bag or a shirt or something in the window," I say. "Something so people know there's not somebody in there."

"Um okay." She leans over her front seat with her back half sticking out of the driver-side door. "Can you get my bag from the trunk?"

Just as I return to the back of the car, she pops the trunk. Ice encrusts it and it takes a good amount of effort to pop it open. When I do, her bag is sitting squarely in the middle.

I toss it over my shoulder and shut the trunk door as she rolls up her window to trap a shopping bag in it.

"Think that'll work?" she asks.

"It's fine. Let's go." Back at my car, I toss Steph's

bag in the backseat, peel off my gloves, and rub my hands together in front of the blasting heaters.

When Steph climbs into the passenger seat, I shift into gear, check over my shoulder, and do a careful U-turn to head back to the house.

"Thanks again for picking me up," she says.

"It's not like I was going to leave you alone," I say. "That's not the type of person I am."

She takes note of the barb. "For what it's worth, I'm sorry for leaving."

"You're just saying that because you got stuck."

"No. I've had time to think and it was really unfair of me to just ditch you like that," she says. "I've been having a great time with you. Honestly, that surprised me. It…scared me a little."

What she says is nice to hear, but I'm not willing to let her off the hook that easily.

She turns and looks out the window on her side. After a deep breath—and nothing from me—she goes on. "Work has been stressing me out lately. I can't trust some people and taking this vacation at such a short notice was…unprofessional, I guess. I was regretting the decision to leave." She laughs in a nervous way. "I know that's totally ridiculous. I work hard. Do a good job. I should be able to take time off during the holidays. And yet here I am obsessing over this. You don't think about this stuff, do you?"

"No," I say pointedly. Then, when she doesn't

reply, I add, "I separate work from my personal life. I don't think of work when I'm not at work and vice versa."

"Oh sure. You compartmentalize. I wish I could do that. But no. It's just constant chatter and worry up here." She taps the side of her head, a little harder than she probably should. The time alone in the car has given her a lot of time to really kick herself for some of her decisions.

We drive in silence for a while, but the whole time my mind is racing. Debating whether I should tell her what's been going on in my life. Unbox the contents of the compartments in my brain. She's let me into her life, albeit reluctantly, so maybe I can trust her with my own.

"My, um, grandfather passed away in the spring." I clear my throat. It's a habit I have that helps me cope with difficult conversations. It's been something I've especially leaned on in the last year.

"Oh," she says. "I'm sorry."

"He and I were really close. After my parents split up, my dad fell out of my life so Mom and I moved in with Grandpa. Then when Mom got sick, he was there for me through it all until after she was gone. The courts couldn't find my dad, and by then I was a teenager so I had a little bit more say in where I was going. And I wanted to stay with my grandfather. We've been inseparable ever since. Well, until last spring."

"Carson, I'm so sorry." Steph reaches over and rubs my shoulder.

I let out a deep breath, pushing away the emotions that have been bubbling up for nearly a year now. "So anyway. This is my first Christmas without anyone and I didn't want to spend it alone in the house I shared with him. I didn't want to spend it alone period, which was why I was actually relieved when I showed up to our Airbnb last weekend and you were there. I was happy for the company."

"We hit it off pretty well, considering."

"Yeah. But when you left, I felt all that loneliness rush back. And what's more is, I realized just how much I've grown used to you. How much I look forward to seeing you every morning. I know it sounds crazy because we've only known each other a few days, but I think I'm starting to —"

"Carson, stop."

I look over at her, then the road, trying to survey what she saw that's oncoming that I've missed. Another car or a deer or something, but there's nothing in front of us but snow.

"What?"

"Don't say it," she tells me. "Let's not cross any lines. Our situation is temporary. W've become friendly, but that's it. We can't let ourselves go someplace we can't come back from."

"But —"

"Just don't," she says. "Nothing will ever happen between us."

She speaks with finality. Like there's no other options. And worse, I understand exactly what she means. We live two different lives in two different worlds. After our vacation is over, we may never see each other again.

But I can't help the way I feel. So instead I keep it to myself. And we drive on in silence.

DECEMBER 22ND
Steph

❄ ❄ ❄

It feels like we're a married couple. Neither Carson nor I have said much to each other yet today. And somehow we both knew exactly how the day was going to pan out. After we were each ready to go for the day, all it took was one word to confirm what we had somehow already figured out on our own.

The drive to pick up my car is awkward. The sun has come out and the roads have mostly been cleared. As we drive, I keep my eyes on the shoulder, trying to gauge how much my car will be buried when we arrive.

Even though Carson and I don't talk, I can tell he's thinking about me and the conversation I made him stop last night. I knew he was about to confess his feelings for me, and I didn't want him to go there. Not when I've been trying to avoid those very same feelings myself.

The problem is, I can't really trust these feelings. Are they real? Do I actually care about him in that way or is this just a product of circumstance? We were thrown together in a weird twist of fate that doesn't happen to normal people. Is it a sign that we were meant to be together or is this connection we feel just because we were suddenly thrust on each other? Until I can be sure, this thing between us is just a fantasy. It's not real life.

As we pull up to my car, I'm relieved to see that it's not too buried. Snow plows have certainly gone by, pushing the snow around my car, but the relentless sun has also allowed the layer of snow on top to melt most of the way.

Carson pulls off to the side of the road as best he can and puts on his four-way flashers.

"Stay here," he grumbles, before he steps out of the warm vehicle. He grabs a snow shovel from the back of his car and starts clearing around mine.

Not wanting to just sit and watch him work, I twist in my seat and look to see if there's another snow shovel so I can help him. There isn't.

It takes Carson about twenty minutes to unbury my car. When he comes back into the car, he buckles up, rests his hand casually on the steering wheel, and looks forward. "You should be okay to get out."

"Thank you," I mutter just before exiting the vehicle myself.

The wind hits me as soon as I step outside, sending a chill right through all of my warm layers. The inside of my car offers no relief, other than the happy feeling I get when my car starts. That feeling only grows when I shift into gear, press my foot to the gas, and feel the car start to pull away as if it had never been stuck to begin with.

I do a U-turn to head back to Batavia and offer Carson a wave as I pass. He keeps his eyes facing forward, turning his car around after I pass so he can follow me.

"You'll talk to me eventually," I say out loud. It's a way of keeping the promise to myself.

The heat finally kicks in about five minutes into my drive, which is also when my phone begins to ring. With the roads clear and the bluetooth switch on my steering wheel, I figure it's okay to take the call.

"Hello?"

"Stephanie? It's Monica from the office. How are you?"

Her voice throws me for a loop. She's the last person I expected to hear on the other end of the phone line. I regret answering it on speakerphone now. Conversations in the car on speakerphone are always awkward. Shouting louder than you need to, muffled responses, a lot of back and forth "Huh?" or "What's that?" Not the most ideal situation to have a conversation with your boss.

But I've already answered, so I try to sound as casual as possible.

"Oh hi. I'm doing okay. How are you?"

"I'm well," she says. "I'm sorry to bother you on your vacation, but I'm afraid I'm calling you with some awkward news."

This isn't like Monica. At least, not that I've ever seen. She never calls a personal number. She never beats around the bush. When I first met her, I thought she was brass, but now I know that kindness doesn't usually register with her. Neither does meanness. She just doesn't think about emotions when she speaks. It is what it is with Monica.

So this conversation is suspicious.

"Oh?" is all that I can muster.

"I wanted to apologize for our last conversation in person," she goes on. "I insinuated that you didn't put in the work and I've recently found out that that wasn't the case."

I squeeze the steering wheel, trying to focus on the road and follow her train of thought at the same time. "I'm confused."

"Richard told me he found the plans I had requested," she explains. "I sent you an email about it."

"Yes, I saw it."

"However, the plans he submitted were incomplete. There were changes that I had remembered the architects had made that weren't in the plans that Richard submitted. So I searched your cubicle and found your notes for the project. They were impressive, as always. Very thorough, which I know you always are. Anyway, the whole thing had me suspicious so I asked IT to show me the cameras and I wasn't too surprised to see Richard going into your cubicle after hours and taking something with him. I searched his desk and found the plans we had discussed with more of your handwritten notes on them."

Although this story seems to be going in my favor, I can't help but feel a little violated that my desk has been invaded twice in my absence without me knowing.

"So you have the plans?" I ask.

"Yes. And I've fired Richard as well. He's been on my radar for a while now, but this was the last straw. So, I was just calling to apologize for the whole thing and to tell you not to worry. I didn't want you to have this stress on your mind through the holidays."

"Thank you." I try to hide my enthusiasm, but I'm not successful. "I appreciate the call."

"You're welcome. Enjoy your time off. Merry Christmas."

"Merry Christmas," I tell her just before she cuts out.

The rest of the drive, I feel like I'm flying. Things at work have straightened out, Richard will no longer be an issue, and I have the rest of the week off.

What more could I possibly want?

My high collapses as soon as I look in my rearview mirror and see Carson's car following behind me. No matter what else I do this week, I need to make things right with him.

DECEMBER 22ND
Steph

✳ ✳ ✳

It's been a couple hours since we've been back at the house and I haven't found a way to break the tension with Carson yet. He always seems to know where I am in the house so he can avoid me. I've tried sitting next to him on the couch, but he just keeps his eyes on his phone and steps out of the room. I've tried talking to him directly, but all I get are one-word responses. I've even asked him point-blank if he's ever going to talk to me again and he just shrugs.

Frankly, I think he's being a bit childish. But I guess I can't blame him. I'm the one standing in the way of us maybe becoming something…even if I know that it won't actually go anywhere. Where have all these emotions come from all of a sudden?

I'm in the kitchen, making myself a peanut butter and jelly sandwich while Carson stokes up the fire in the fireplace. The kitchen floor feels cold on my toes, so I quickly finish what I'm doing so I can leave the room. I step across the hardwoods to put the knife in the sink, but stop when a thought occurs to me.

Returning to my prep space on the counter, I pull out two more slices of bread and prepare a second sandwich. PB&J is comfort food for me, so maybe it will help me bridge the gap with Carson. The dude's gotta be getting hungry with as much as he's been avoiding me all day.

After I make the sandwich and clean up the crumbs, I set the two sandwiches on a plate and carry it out to the living room, where Carson is sitting on the couch in front of the roaring fire and the twinkle of the Christmas lights.

"I made us dinner."

He keeps his eyes on his phone. "No thanks."

"You didn't even look at what it is," I say. "This is gourmet stuff."

His eyes flicker up and a reluctant smile spreads across his face. "A sandwich?"

"Ah," I hold up a finger. "It's peanut butter and jelly on wheat. And this isn't the generic stuff. It's Peter Pan and Welch's. Top shelf quality right here."

He hooks an eyebrow, still grinning. "Oh? What about the bread?"

"The bread is simply the vehicle for the flavor."

"So you skimped on this meal?"

I let out an exasperated sigh. "Just take the damn sandwich already!"

He reaches up and takes his from the plate. I sit beside him, balance the plate on my knees, and eat mine.

"PB&J for the win again."

"Huh?" he asks.

"It's the only way I could get you to talk to me. It's a miracle sandwich."

"Okay, now you're taking it too far."

"But it worked."

He studies his half-eaten sandwich. "Yeah, I guess it did."

"I understand why you're upset with me—"

"I'm not upset with *you*. Just the situation."

"Either way, I get it," I say. "It probably feels like I'm rejecting you. I just want you to know that I'm not."

He keeps his eyes on the floor. "Sounded that way to me."

I sigh. "You have to understand that I never intended to meet anyone. Not anyone that I really like, at least."

Carson looks up at me, hope in his eyes. "I really like you too."

I can't help but smile at that. "I'm not from here, so I guess I always had this thought that I might move back home eventually. I just feel like if I were to get into a relationship here in New York that I'd feel stuck here and I wouldn't return home. Where my family is."

"I can see that," he says in a small voice. He tears off the crust from the second half on his sandwich.

"But it's different with you."

"How so?"

I squirm. I've never liked talking about how I feel. It makes me vulnerable and exposed. And stupid. "With you I feel safe. Comfortable. At home." I look over at him to see him smiling wide. I shoot to my feet and step closer to the fire. "And that scares me!"

"Steph." He comes closer, resting his hand on my back. "I'm not asking you to marry me. Last night I was just trying to be honest about how I feel. I like you. And, if you're willing, I'd like to give this a shot. I'd like to give *us* a shot." His arms wrap around me.

I turn and face him. "I think…" I take a deep breath and jump right in. "I think I'd like that too."

Without a moment to spare, he pulls me in for a kiss. In that moment, alone in the house we stumbled into together, the rush of the fire, and the twinkle of the Christmas lights, I feel like everything is going to be perfectly okay.

CHRISTMAS EVE
Carson

❄ ❄ ❄

The shops downtown are few, but Steph and I still want to check them out. Over the last week, we have both scoped them out individually, but it's better when you can share it with someone else. Besides, we both agree that we need something memorable to mark the occasion that is Christmas Eve. What better way to do that than to support some small businesses?

"Books and Bakes," Steph says as we make our way down Jackson Street. "I've been meaning to stop in here, but haven't yet. Want to check it out?"

"Sure." I tuck my coat tighter around my neck as the wind cuts across the parking lot from across the street. Maybe someday that big empty plot of asphalt will be occupied by buildings to block these bitter gusts and give the street extra charm. Until then, the stores present a refuge from the weather.

The front door is wooden, one of the traditional storefronts that was built during the city's heyday. There's an "Open" sign hanging in the window. The bell above the door jingles when we step in.

"Welcome to Books and Bakes," a man says from behind the counter to our left. "Are you looking for something specific?"

The walls are lined with books. Bestsellers, mostly, but there are some quirky souvenir-type titles by the register, just beside the glass case displaying all of the delicious baked goods. There are two dining tables in each of the windows on either side of the door, and plush furniture is situated by the bookshelves. There's a lot of stuff in here for such a small shop, but the place doesn't seem cramped at all.

"We're just checking things out," Steph explains.

"We're from out-of-town," I add. "We're staying at an Airbnb on Clinton Street."

The man nods. "I see. Decided to come to Batavia for its small town charm?"

Steph smiles and looks up at me. "We both needed an escape."

"This is the perfect place to do it. I'm Jeff." He extends his hand across the counter for us to shake and we introduce ourselves. "I'm the co-owner. My girlfriend, Lexi, is cleaning up the kitchen in back. Might I interest you in a plate of our cookies?

They're half-off, seeing as it's almost closing time and we'll have to toss them before we leave."

Steph examines all of the options. "They do look delicious. But I can't decide."

"I'll tell you what: I'll put together a variety pack for you while you shop."

"Perfect," she says with another smile. "Thank you."

I eye up the mysteries along the back wall and pull one from the shelf to read the back. Steph moves along to the shelf down the wall and inspects another book.

After a few minutes, she comes up beside me and asks, "Are you going to get anything?"

"I think so," I say. "Are you ready?"

"We should probably get back ourselves and let these guys go on home."

I walk up to the counter and set me book down beside the plate of Christmas cookies that Jeff has packaged up for Steph.

"All set?" Jeff asks.

"I think so," I tell him. "Are we your last customers?"

"Last ones for the day." Jeff punches our purchases into the register. "We're closing up for Christmas as soon as you guys leave."

"Oh, then we'd better hurry." Steph fishes for bills from her wallet. I start to refuse, but she shoots me a look. I paid for dinner, so this is her way of thanking me. "We weren't sure you'd be open today."

"Neither did we." Jeff takes her money. As he hands Steph her change, he says, "But Lexi wanted to get the rest of the dishes cleaned up and I figured we might as well put the 'Open' sign up and see who wanders in."

"I'm glad you did," I tell him as I take the paper bag from him that holds our purchases. "You have a great shop. Books and baked goods, count me in."

Jeff laughs with a genuine smile. "Merging both of our interests."

"Have a nice day and a merry Christmas!" Steph leads us to the door.

"Thanks again!" I call out to him as I follow Steph back out into the cold.

The snow has slowed, but it's still falling. We walk back to where we parked on Bank Street, not really talking much as we brace ourselves in the cold wind.

Back at the house, we hang up our coats and Steph steps toward the kitchen.

"I think we could both use some hot chocolate," she says. "Spiked?"

I shrug. "Doesn't matter. Surprise me."

As she disappears into the kitchen, I sneak up to my room and retrieve the box I bought for her a few days ago. By time I return, Steph is carrying two mugs out to the living room.

"Which holiday classic will we be watching tonight?" she asks.

"*Home Alone*?"

"Perfect. Maybe we'll even have time to watch the second one tonight too." She sits on the couch and pulls a blanket over her. "Are you coming?"

I step toward her and present the box.

Her eyes flicker up from the box to mine. "This isn't an engagement ring, is it? You said—"

"It's not an engagement ring—or jewelry of any sort."

"I didn't get you anything."

"It doesn't matter. I saw this and thought that you'd like it."

She still looks concerned, so I push her more.

"Just open it!"

She takes it from me and unwraps it. As soon as she sees what's inside, she throws her head back and laughs. "Where on *earth* did you get this?" She pulls up the peanut butter and jelly sandwich ornament and examines it.

"One of the shops downtown. Do you like it?"

"I love it." She leans over and kisses me. "It perfectly sums up our week and how easily you cave to a PB&J." She stands and hangs her gift on one of the tree branches.

"Uh, that's not exactly what happened."

"Sure it is." She returns to the couch and grabs the remote.

"No, what happened is—"

"Shh! The movie's starting."

I smirk and settle in next to her, warming as she leans into me. This Christmas turned out completely different than I thought it would be. There was no family, no gifts, and yet it turned out perfectly. I wouldn't want it any other way.

A chance moment. A snow storm. And the gift of a new beginning.

Tristan is ready to party and ring in the New Year by kissing his soon-to-be girlfriend, Julie. The only bad note in his rocking night is the ongoing snow storm. Outside his apartment, he's almost hit by a swerving car! Behind the wheel is Grace, the most beautiful woman with haunting green eyes. She's on her own mission to get home to her grandfather.

In a selfless act reminiscent of the age of knights and chivalry, Tristan vows to get her home…never realizing they are both on a date with destiny and their lives will be forever changed by the SNOW AFTER CHRISTMAS…

More by the Author

To find more books by the author, visit
DavidNethBooks.com/Books

* * *

Subscribe to his newsletter to be the first to know of new
releases and special deals!
DavidNethBooks.com/Newsletter

* * *

If you enjoyed the book, please consider leaving a review
on Goodreads or the retailer you bought it from. Reviews
help potential readers determine whether they'll enjoy a
book, so any comments on what you thought of the story
would be very helpful!

ABOUT THE AUTHOR

D. Allen is the author of the sweet small town romance series, Montana Beach and Small Town Christmas.

Also writes fantasy and superhero fiction as David Neth.

www.DavidNethBooks.com
www.facebook.com/DavidNethBooks

www.ingramcontent.com/pod-product-compliance
Lightning Source LLC
Chambersburg PA
CBHW030806190726
48285CB00003B/1050